Murder on a High Note

Music Shop Mysteries, Book 1

Jennifer Lamont Leo

Mountain Majesty Media

MURDER ON A HIGH NOTE

Published by Mountain Majesty Media, Inc.

PO Box 638, Cocolalla, Idaho 83813

ISBN: 979-8-9901647-1-0 (e-book)

ISBN: 979-8-9901647-2-7 (paperback)

ISBN: 979=8-9901647-4-1 (large print)

Copyright © 2025 by Jennifer Lamont Leo

Cover Design by Dee Dee Book Covers

Library of Congress Cataloging-in-Publication Data

Leo, Jennifer Lamont

Murder on a High Note/Jennifer Lamont Leo 1st ed.

Printed in the United States of America

Chapter One

On that steamy June Saturday in 1916, not even the sweat pooling under my white cotton blouse could dampen my mood. Summer had come at last to Timber Coulee, Idaho— a joy not taken for granted in this small mountain town near the Canadian border.

With summertime came music-camp season.

And with music-camp season came the saving grace of my little music shop.

What Christmastime was to other retailers, camp season was to me. My busiest time of year, when the ledger would start to show black ink instead of red, and I could breathe easy that the rent would be paid and the electricity remain connected.

The bell above the door of Mountain Melodies gave a merry jangle as I pushed my way in, arms laden with a heavy shipment of gramophone records lugged from the Timber Coulee post office. The familiar scent of lemon polish and aged wood enveloped me as I navigated the maze of pianos, cellos, and other musical instruments. Sunlight streamed through the display windows and glinted off the polished brass of trumpets and saxophones mounted on the walls.

"Ernie? Are you still here?" With an unladylike grunt, I deposited my burden on the counter and unpinned my straw hat, which I hung on a peg on the wall. If the temperature continued to climb, we'd have to prop open the door and plug in the electric fan—not my preferred solution, since breezes blew the sheet music around, but the store could become stifling otherwise, and humidity wasn't good for the instruments.

A muffled thump followed by a colorful curse answered me. From behind the towering lid of a baby grand piano emerged Ernie Weiss, rubbing his curly gray head.

"Land's sakes, Amanda Parrish," he grumbled. "You trying to scare years off my life?" The town's handyman, piano tuner, and all-around fixer of everything was seventy if he was a day, but still moved with the grace of a younger man. His well-worn blue denim overalls hung comfortably on his tall frame, the fabric softened by years of use and laundering. Smile lines etched his weathered face and deepened when he grinned, as he was doing now.

I reached for a tin on a high shelf. "If I haven't managed that in all these years, I doubt I'll start now. Peppermint?"

He accepted the proffered candy in a hand callused from a lifetime of work. "Much obliged. Now, about this stubborn piano—"

"Oh, take a break from that old thing," I interrupted. "Come and see these new gramophone records I've just gotten in. Look, the New York Philharmonic, with Stuart von Bauer conducting." I picked up one thick shellac disk and examined the photograph on its paper envelope, a heavy-jowled man holding a baton aloft. "Just think of it! The great maestro himself will be right here in little Timber Coulee, conducting the Camp Harmony orchestra and teaching the strings program."

Ernie's bushy eyebrows rose. "A fancy orchestra conductor from New York City? Hmpf. Probably thinks he's too good for our little town."

"Now, now. Mr. von Bauer is a true artist. A world-class conductor and violin virtuoso. Just think of all he'll teach the campers! People will want to buy his recordings. And heaven knows my little store could use the income. We barely stayed afloat through the winter."

"Too soon to panic," Ernie said. "I mean, isn't summer usually the store's busiest season?"

"Who's panicking? Of course, we rely on the music camp to boost our sales every summer. All I'm saying is, there's a lot of red ink in the ledger, and we need to get back in the black. I predict these Victrola records will sell faster than Esther Mulligan's peach pie at a church social, once the word gets out."

"Speaking of word getting out, didn't some big national magazine run an article about the camp?" Ernie asked. "This being the big anniversary and all. Dinah was telling me about it."

"That's right." From a drawer beneath the counter I pulled out the June 1916 copy of *Metronome*, the leading music-industry magazine. "My copy came in the mail a few days ago. I set it aside to read later, then forgot all about it." I flipped through the pages. "Here it is. 'Rural Idaho's Camp Harmony Celebrates Silver Jubilee.' Oh, look! There's a picture of you and Carrie Tate holding a rake and a shovel, standing in front of a tulip bed. Listen to the caption. It says, 'Mr. Ernie Weiss and Mrs. Michael Tate spruce up Camp Harmony in preparation of its twenty-fifth anniversary.' Ernie, you're famous!"

He came around the piano and peered over my shoulder. "I remember some photographer poking around the grounds early last spring. Took a bunch of pictures of me spreading fertilizer and whatnot." He snorted. "I said to myself, what's this fellow really interested in, music or landscaping?"

"It's because you're so photogenic. And look, so is Mr. von Bauer." I pointed to a portrait of the serious white-haired man sporting a large medallion on a striped ribbon around his neck. "My, my. So distinguished-looking."

"Sourpuss, if you ask me," Ernie grumped. "Probably stepped off the train, took one look at Timber Coulee, and wondered what he'd gotten himself into."

"Oh, stop. He must already be in town, since he'll be the guest of honor at the patrons' banquet tonight." A bolt of euphoria shot through me. "I can't wait to meet him. You are coming, aren't you? To the banquet, I mean."

"Yes, ma'am, I'll be there, but I'll be working behind the scenes, in the kitchen. That old stove is on its last legs, so I promised Dinah I'd be on hand with my toolbox in case it starts acting up. Can't have anything go wrong at such an important celebration."

"Someone's in the kitchen with Dinah," I sang. As it happened, the cook's name really was Dinah, and her hatred of that old folksong was legendary. Nobody familiar with it would dare hum it in her presence. Away from the camp kitchen, however, it was a rather lame joke among those of us who knew her.

Normally, the remark would have elicited a chuckle, but Ernie's mind seemed elsewhere. Was he really that worried about the stove?

"I'm sure Carrie and Michael will appreciate your efforts," I continued. "Dinah's a bit high-strung to begin with, isn't she? A finicky stove during a major event might cause her to snap."

"Oh, she'll be all right." Ernie sighed, his shoulders slumping. "But speaking of high-strung, that blasted Leon Danvers was at my door again this morning."

Struggling to keep pace with the abrupt change in topic, I set aside the magazine. "That real estate developer from back East? New Century something or other? What did he want this time?"

"Same as always," Ernie grumbled, his face darkening. "Trying to buy my house out from under me. Says he's got grand plans for some fancy new hotel. Can you imagine? Tearing down perfectly good homes in order to build a skyscraper? Six stories tall, he tells me. Six! What does our little town need with a building that tall?"

"I suppose we ought to be thankful. I've heard the Woolworth Building in New York has sixty." I paused to let that startling fact sink in. "Even so, I agree that buildings that size don't belong in Timber Coulee. Besides, we already have a perfectly good hotel in town that's more than adequate. That man has no shame. Did you tell him to leave you alone?"

A bit of sparkle returned to his eyes. "Oh, I told him, all right. Said I'd sooner live in a chicken coop than sell to the likes of him."

"Good for you, Ernie." I patted his arm. "Don't let that snake bully you. If he continues to bother you, perhaps you should inform the sheriff."

"Oh, I'm sure the sheriff's got enough on his plate already, with all that vandalism going on around town."

"Vandalism?" I gave him a curious glance. "What vandalism?"

"All that anti-German rubbish. Businesses getting rocks thrown through their windows, nasty messages painted on walls. Where you been, girl?"

"I've been busy getting this shop ready for the onslaught of music-campers, that's what." Then I dropped my defensive attitude. As a Main Street merchant, this unwelcome news concerned me. Vandalism could ruin my shop. Further, it might bring bad publicity to the town, even worse during music camp season. "How many businesses have been affected?"

"Don't know, exactly. A few. And not only the Germans, but other foreigners as well. Mr. Ching's vegetable cart was overturned at the market two days ago. Cabbages everywhere."

"How awful. I hope the sheriff finds out who's doing it, and quick.

But you be careful."

Ernie pointed at his chest. "Me? I'm an American. My family's been in America for generations."

"I didn't mean that. I mean, it sounds like Leon Danvers might be out to make trouble for you in his zeal to obtain your property."

"I can take care of myself. But Leon's not just after my place, you know." Ernie lowered his voice, even though we were the only two in the room. "Poor Heidi from Elite Repeat is getting the same treatment. She lives next door to me, and Danvers wants her house as much as he wants mine. Saw her looking mighty upset yesterday."

A pang of worry for my friend shot through me. "Oh, dear. I'll have to check on her. That Danvers fellow is becoming a real menace to our community. If there's something I can do to help, please let me know."

"Just listen to me moan and groan, I expect," Ernie said. "And try not to give Leon Danvers the time of day."

"I won't." As Ernie dove back under the piano lid, I surveyed Mountain Melodies with pride, imagining it filled with the vibrant energy of musicians young and old. The camp season was more than just a boon to my business—it was a time when Timber Coulee transformed from a sleepy lumber town to a center for the musical arts, a place where melodies blossomed and friendships were forged. And I was more than happy to serve the musicians' many needs. It would be a daunting challenge to manage the shop single-handedly this summer, but a reinforcement was on her way. Business would pick up—as long as nobody threw a rock through my window.

"Better stock up on rosin." I jotted a list on a notepad next to the cash register. "And maybe some earplugs, for the teachers' sake."

A soft mewling broke through my reverie. Moxie, the orange tabby cat who ruled over the shop, perched atop the ancient piano bench next to Ernie. His eyes were half-closed in contentment as he stretched one lazy paw out before tucking it back against his fluffy chest.

"Well, Moxie." I crossed the room to join him. "Are you ready for the summer rush too? Or are you just planning to nap your way through it all?"

Moxie blinked up at me, his tail whisking back and forth, granting permission for me to scratch behind his ears. "It looks like we're in for a musical whirlwind soon. Are you ready to greet all the new faces and maybe steal a few heartwarming pats on the head?"

Moxie responded with a dignified meow before leaping onto the polished counter, his fluffy tail swishing as he settled in a sunbeam streaming through the window. He glanced at me with a regal air, as if to say that of course he was ready for any attention that came his way.

Amused at his royal demeanor, I returned to my task of sorting the gramophone records.

"Your niece'll be here soon, right?" Ernie said from within the piano. "Bet you're mighty excited about that."

"Next week." My spirit lifted at the thought of my summer house-guest, who'd also offered to help run the shop. "She'll be arriving just about the time camp gets underway."

"Is she gonna participate this year?"

"Well, at nineteen she's too old to be an official camper. But I told Carrie Tate she might like to help out in some capacity, when she's not busy here in the shop. And as a serious music student, I know she'd love to participate in the orchestra, if Maestro von Bauer will allow it."

"He will, if he knows what's good for him. Apple doesn't fall far from the tree, I reckon. She play as well as you did?"

"Better, if you can believe it." Memories of my cello-playing days, before a chronic wrist injury put that career to rest, brought on a slight pang of nostalgia. "I'm looking forward to getting to know her as a young adult. She was a child the last time we saw each other."

Ernie grunted.

Abandoning my task, I picked up one of the gramophone records, and carried it to the Victrola machine in the corner. I wound it up, set the needle, and soon the shop hummed with the crackling notes of a lively Mozart concerto.

"That's some mighty fine fiddling." Ernie's voice floated over the gentle tinkering of his tools as he tightened the last tuning pin.

"But secretly you'd prefer 'Turkey in the Straw.'" I flashed him a smile.

Ernie chuckled and wiped his brow with a rag pulled from the pocket of his well-worn overalls.

Grabbing a letter opener and turning to the rest of the morning's mail. I sliced open the white envelope lying on top of the pile and unfolded the crisp paper inside. My eyes darted across the typewritten lines. Then I read it again, more slowly this time. With each word, blood pounded in my temples. The letter, addressed to me as a board member of Camp Harmony, made a shocking request in ugly terms. Instead of a signature, there was only a single word at the bottom. *Anonymous*. I grabbed the envelope for another look, but it bore no information other than a Timber Coulee postmark and my name and address. I sank onto a nearby stool, the letter trembling in my hands as its contents settled over me like a suffocating blanket. The ugliness of the words seemed to poison the very air of my cheerful shop.

"Something the matter?" Ernie's voice was laced with concern.

I smoothed out the crumpled paper. If I couldn't trust old Ernie Weiss, who could I trust? "It's an anonymous letter to the Camp Harmony board. They're demanding we disinvite Stuart von Bauer because he's German." My voice caught. "They're calling him a potential spy, an enemy combatant. They even have the gall to question the camp board's patriotism."

Ernie's eyes widened. "Well, I'll be. That's a load of hogwash if I ever heard one."

"It's not just hogwash, it's dangerous." I stood and paced behind the counter, Mozart's bright notes now seeming to mock the darkness of human nature. "First rocks through windows, then overturned vegetable carts, and now this? Where does it end?"

The letter shook in my hands as I remembered my grandmother's stories of fleeing persecution in the old country, of doors slammed in faces, of neighbors turning against neighbors.

"It's fear talking," Ernie shook his head. "War makes people do and say foolish things."

"But that's just it." I stood and paced behind the counter. "The U.S. isn't even involved in the war. Not yet, anyway. And President Wilson has promised to keep us out of it, hasn't he? In any case, we can't let fear dictate our actions." Words seemed inadequate. "Music is supposed to bring people together, Ernie. That's what Camp Harmony has always been about."

Ernie huffed. "Wouldn't surprise me if one of those flag-waving jingoists in the Liberty League wrote it."

"I suppose it's possible, but unlikely. Seems to me those in the League are too busy selling war bonds, hosting patriotic sing-alongs, and selling flag buttons to compose anonymous poison-pen letters. Not that any of those things are wrong, mind you. I'm patriotic, myself. But some members take it too far into downright bigotry against anyone born anyplace other than the forty-eight states." I set the offensive epistle aside. "Come to think of it, a more extreme Liberty League member wouldn't want to stay anonymous. He or she'd be quite proud of demanding that a German-born conductor be fired."

His wrinkled forehead creased even more. "So what are you going to do about it?"

Determination set in. "Well, first, I'm going to have to discuss it with the rest of the board, as well as the Tates. We need to address this head-on. I won't stand for this kind of prejudice in our community, especially not at our camp. Think of the bad publicity." To be honest, my concerns weren't one-hundred-percent altruistic. Bad publicity for the camp could mean sagging profits for Mountain Melodies.

"Good for you." Ernie's proud smile spread across his weathered face. "You've always had a good head on your shoulders. The camp's lucky to have you on the board."

"Flattery will get you a free set of guitar strings." Feeling better now that I had a plan, I tossed him a wink. "And maybe even a discount on that banjo you've been eyeing."

"Deal!" The lines around his eyes crinkled with genuine delight.

Dear Ernie. I could always count on his support. "In all seriousness, Ernie, thank you. It means a lot to hear you say that." My eye caught the article in *Metronome*, still lying open on the counter. "But if Timber Coulee is lucky to have anyone, it's Carrie and Michael Tate. Without them, the music camp would have never come about in the first place. I dread to think how they'll react to the accusation that they're un-American for inviting Mr. von Bauer. But enough of that for now." I glanced at the wall clock. "Let's get this place shipshape. The campers are coming, and we can't have Molly thinking her aunt runs a shoddy establishment."

We returned to our tasks, my mind already whirling with plans. I'd fight this prejudice with every ounce of my being. Camp Harmony would live up to its name, bringing people together through the universal language of music. And Stuart von Bauer would be there to lead the way, German heritage and all.

The battle against fear and prejudice wouldn't be easy, but with music as our ally, I was certain we would prevail.

Chapter Two

After Ernie left, I flipped the sign on the door to Closed and popped around the corner to my little yellow house, where I took a quick bath and pinned up my hair. In the mirror a few more silver strands sparkled among the brown, but not to fret. After all, at thirty-five, what could one expect? At least my face remained relatively unlined for such an advanced age.

My one-and-only formal dress, a floor-length, sapphire-blue silk gown that I'd had since my Chicago days, would have to do for the evening. The dress looked a bit dated now—the puffed sleeves gave it an Edwardian air, and ladies' magazines these days were featuring ankle-length gowns—but the color was my favorite and there was no need to replace it yet. Few events called for fancy dresses in Timber Coulee, but tonight's banquet was a very special occasion, a thank-you of sorts for the loyal patrons and supporters of Camp Harmony, just prior to the camp's seasonal opening.

The local sheriff and my good friend, James Holcomb, had offered to give me a lift to the event. Although the noisy Dodge sedan with "Sheriff's Department" emblazoned on the doors lacked elegance, it spared me the even more humbling experience of riding up the mountain aboard the mule-drawn lumber wagon temporarily repurposed as transport between town and camp.

"That's a mighty pretty dress." James helped me into the passenger seat, his eyes lingering appreciatively on the blue silk ruffles. "Makes your eyes sparkle like Lake Collier in July." He cleared his throat and looked away, suddenly very interested in adjusting the side-view mirror. I smoothed the fabric over my knees, pleased by the compliment but also aware of the slight awkwardness that had crept into our longtime friendship lately. Ever since his wife, Sarah, had passed the previous winter, these little moments of attention had been happening more frequently, and I wasn't quite sure how I felt about that.

As we bumped along the road, the cool evening air whipping through my carefully styled hair, it seemed a good time to broach the subject that had been weighing on my mind.

"James." I shifted in my seat to face him. "Have you heard that there's a movement afoot to have Stuart von Bauer banished from leading the music camp this year because he's German?"

His brow furrowed as he kept his eyes on the winding road. "Yeah, I heard about it. Darn shame. Where'd you hear about it?"

"I received an anonymous letter in this morning's mail. Presumably the other camp board members did, too. Do you know who might have sent it?" A flicker of hope ignited in my chest that soon we'd get to the bottom of this foolishness and bring the coward to justice. *Anonymous*, indeed, lacking even the courage to take responsibility for his or her unpopular stance.

James set his jaw. "I'm afraid not. These kinds of incidents have been happening all over town with increasing regularity. Harassment, vandalism..."

The flicker of hope sputtered. "All over town? But why?"

"Fear, mostly," James voice was tight. "With the war in Europe, some folks are getting riled up against anyone they see as 'foreign.' Germans are getting the worst of it, but it's not just them."

"That's terrible." So much worse than what Ernie had described. No matter our personal faults and foibles, Timber Coulee folks had always looked out for one another. What was happening to my little town? "What is being done about it?"

James's knuckles whitened on the steering wheel. "As sheriff, I can tell you my team and I are working our tails off trying to find the culprits. But it's not easy. These cowards strike at random, at night, and so far, no one's been willing to talk."

My stomach churned at the thought of what was happening in our once-peaceful town. "I saw something in the newspaper about the federal government establishing internment camps for Germans. Is that true?" My voice wavered slightly, thinking of the Muellers, the Schmidts, the Webers – families whose Christmas cookies I'd eaten, whose businesses I'd patronized, whose children I'd outfitted with trumpets and gramophone records.

James was quiet for a moment before responding, the silence heavy between us. I studied his profile, searching for some reassurance in the face of the man I'd known since I'd first arrived in Timber Coulee, the one who'd always stood for what was right. But there was a new tension in his jaw that hadn't been there a few months ago.

"It's... complicated," he finally said in a carefully measured tone. "There are camps, yes. But it's not as simple as rounding up all Germans. The camps are meant for spies and other people who mean to do harm to America from within our borders."

I turned to look out the window, not wanting James to see the tears threatening to form. Who would decide who was a spy? What proof would they need? I thought of Mr. Weber, who still spoke with a thick accent despite thirty years in America, who had lost a son in the Battle on San Juan Hill. Would that be enough to prove his loyalty? Or would his weekly letters to his sister in Stuttgart mark him as suspicious?

"You haven't heard anything from your German customers or their families, have you?" James asked, glancing at me sideways. "Any talk that seems... out of place?"

The question hit me like a physical blow. Was James asking me to spy on my own customers? I refused to believe that of him. "They're Americans, James. They love this country as much as we do. Maybe more, because they chose it."

But even as I spoke, I wondered how many others in town would see it that way. How many would choose fear over faith in their neighbors? And how long before suspicion turned to something worse?

"I know. And as sheriff, I'm doing my best to protect everyone in this town, regardless of where they come from. But I can't be everywhere at once."

Sensing his frustration, I backed off. The job of sheriff was never easy, even at the best of times, and these were far from the best of times. The world I thought I knew seemed to be changing rapidly, and not for the better.

"We're almost there." James broke through my reverie. "Let's try to enjoy the banquet, Amanda. We all need a little normalcy these days."

"You're right." But as the arched entrance to Camp Harmony came into view, I couldn't shake the feeling that nothing about these times was normal at all.

Camp Harmony lay a good distance from town on the rocky slope of Huckleberry Mountain, nestled in the embrace of towering pines, their evergreen scent mingling with the crisp mountain air.

James parked the sedan and we followed the well-dressed crowd along a needle-strewn path.

The main lodge, an imposing structure of rough-hewn logs and river stone, stood tall at the center of the camp. As James and I climbed the steps to the wide porch, I thanked him for giving me a lift.

He grinned. "Always happy to be of service."

We parted ways at the door. He stayed on the porch to join a group of his law-enforcement colleagues, while I went inside to search for my place card.

To my delight, Camp Harmony's rustic dining hall had been transformed into an elegant banquet room, adorned with banks of flowers and colorful banners proclaiming the camp's Silver Jubilee. Lanterns on every table illuminated the crowd, everyone dressed in their Sunday best. The guests' excited chatter filled the room, while the musicians on stage tuned their instruments. The air was thick with anticipation, along with the tantalizing aromas wafting from the kitchen. The cook might have been a temperamental person to contend with, but she sure could work magic with a kettle and saucepan. The floral centerpieces also emitted a pleasant scent, mixing with the fragrant perfumes worn by the guests.

I was still searching for my place card when Carrie Tate pulled me aside, anxiety deepening the wrinkles on her face.

"I have the most dreadful news," she stage-whispered. "Everything happened so quickly, I didn't even have time to alert you board members."

"What is it?" Would she be able to shed some light on the troubling anonymous letter?

"Stuart von Bauer has canceled his appearance. Left us completely in the lurch."

My mouth fell open. "What? He can't do that," I sputtered. "We have a contract."

"We do. But apparently, he's taken ill, quite suddenly, and his doctor forbade him to travel, much less work at the camp for the entire season."

Deep disappointment roiled my stomach, along with concern for the camp. I'd been so looking forward to meeting the illustrious conductor. "Oh, Carrie. And camp's supposed to start next week. What are you and Michael going to do?" As owners and directors, the responsibility was theirs to make sure the camp ran like a clock, although of course we board members would pitch in where we could.

She glanced distractedly around the room. "We were able to secure a substitute at the last minute. A Mr. Dieter Volkov." She spoke the name syllable by syllable, as if practicing the pronunciation.

"Dieter Vo-what? Who's that?"

Carrie wrung her hands. "I was afraid you'd say that. Nobody knows who he is. We only just met him this afternoon, when he arrived on the train. Supposedly, he's a competent violinist." She did not sound very confident of this fact.

"Where'd you find him?" Orchestra conductors didn't materialize out of nowhere. Not in Timber Coulee, anyway.

"When von Bauer's agent telephoned from New York, he said he was sending this other fellow, who was recommended to him. Michael and I were stuck between a rock and a hard place. We felt we had to accept, under the circumstances. I mean, the gentleman was already on his way here. And where would our orchestra be without a conductor? Plus, the agent lowered his fee."

My spirits dimmed. "I suppose that was decent of him and all, and I also suppose somebody's better than nobody, but ..." What else could I say? No Stuart von Bauer? I'd been looking forward to meeting him for months! And all those gramophone records I'd invested in for the shop. In my mind's eye, dollar bills whisked out the front door of Mountain Melodies and blew away down the street. Dollars I could ill afford to lose.

My face must have radiated my disappointment, because Carrie's lower lip trembled. "I know. He's a complete unknown without any of the drawing power of a big name. We were counting on von Bauer's fame to help us pack the auditorium at the grand finale concert." She took a deep breath. "And yet, it's a real blessing that this other fellow has stepped up. I mean, how bad could he be? He must be pretty talented, if the agent recommended him. Right? Agents don't recommend just anyone."

"True." *Unless they're worried about collecting their fee.* But, who knew, maybe the man would at least prove competent enough to teach and conduct, even if no one had ever heard of him.

"Second," Carrie continued, "we can afford him. His fee fits into the camp budget better than von Bauer's did."

Ah, yes. Money was always a concern. Camp Harmony tried to keep its costs reasonable so young musicians from all walks of life could afford to attend. Hiring someone as prominent as von Bauer had been a special splurge for the Silver Jubilee, not a regular occurrence. To pay a lower fee would ease the financial strain on the camp budget.

"And third, to be honest, we'd never be able to get anyone else to fill in at the last minute." Carrie shrugged. "We'd probably have to cancel or cut back on the strings program and have no one at all to conduct the symphony. Beggars can't be choosers." Her voice wobbled as if she might burst into tears at any moment.

Poor Carrie! What she needed in this moment was support, not criticism. And certainly not a discussion of the upsetting letter. That could wait until later.

I forced the corners of my mouth to turn upward. "What else do you know about this Dieter fellow?"

"Not much more than I've told you. The agent said he plays with a symphony in Ohio. Oh, and he's Russian. Apparently, he escaped St. Petersburg in the wake of some kind of violent uprising. So he hasn't been in the States very long. But surely, he must have talent, because—"

I held up a hand. "I know. Because the agent recommended him." What was done, was done. "Don't you worry, Carrie. We'll be sure to give him a warm Camp Harmony welcome. You can count on us."

Carrie brightened. "I'm happy to hear you say that, because I've seated him next to you at dinner."

"You've what?" Still reeling over the loss of Stuart von Bauer, the last thing I wanted was small talk all evening with some two-bit Russian fiddler who probably didn't even speak English.

"Please, Amanda." Carrie pressed her hands together under her chin. "You're so good at setting people at ease, and you're able to talk shop with a professional musician. I know you'll treat him with tact and grace." Her gaze rested on the back of Mildred Abernathy's silver head. "Not everyone is capable of that."

"All right," I hissed. "But you owe me."

Carrie took my hand and squeezed it before scurrying off.

I found my seat and greeted the others gathered around the table. While waiting for the Volga Virtuoso to make his appearance, I turned to Oscar Barrington, a fellow board member as well as a manager at the Goldwood Corporation, the region's largest lumber operation.

"Oscar, I hear there are plans for a new hotel to be built in Timber Coulee." Maybe if I kept as neutral a voice as possible, I'd find out what he knew about it.

"Yup." Oscar was a man of few words.

"Is there really a need for a new hotel?" I pressed. "The current hotel is already the largest structure in town, and it looks to be in fine condition."

While Oscar gave me a doleful look, his chatty wife, Martha, spoke up. "Oh, that old thing is thirty years old if it's a day." She wrinkled her nose as if detecting a bad smell. "A glamorous new hotel will attract more tourists. It will be the pride of Timber Coulee, six stories tall. A skyscraper, really. With all the latest modern amenities, and a tower on top that will be capable of transmitting radio signals."

I'd read an article about this thing called radio, some new technology the military was experimenting with. Why a hotel would need a skyscraper with the capacity to transmit radio signals escaped me—and escaped my mouth before I could rein in the words.

"We must make room for progress, Amanda." Martha's tone indicated I alone was blocking Timber Coulee from entering the modern era.

"Progress is well and good, but the developers ought not to pressure people into selling their homes to make room for it."

"I'm sure I don't know what you're talking about." Martha sniffed. "Surely you're exaggerating. In any case, that's something you'd need to address with Leon Danvers. Oscar tells me he's the agent in charge of procuring the land for the New Century Development Corporation."

"Maybe I'll do just that. Is he here?" The gregarious businessman should have been glad-handing his way around the roomful of influential townspeople. Banquet or not, I was ready to give him an earful on behalf of Ernie, Heidi, and anyone else who was being pressured to sell their properties.

"I haven't seen him." Martha turned away to talk to someone else at the table, putting an end to our conversation and leaving me stewing in fresh indignation.

At last, Carrie Tate approached the platform with an air of brave resignation, like Anne Boleyn ascending the scaffold. She clinked a glass for attention and welcomed the crowd. Then her voice faltered. "I'm afraid I have some bad news. To our great regret, Stuart von Bauer is unable to join us this year due to a sudden and severe illness that has left him incapacitated."

A murmur rolled through the crowd. The dismay in the room was palpable, but Carrie soldiered on.

"However, I have some good news, as well. I'm pleased to announce that Mr. Dieter Volkov of the Cleveland Symphony Orchestra has joined us. Mr. Volkov is a respected violinist and skilled conductor who has graciously agreed to fill Maestro von Bauer's place. We are very grateful to him for stepping in at the last moment." With a theatrical flair she extended her arm toward a dinner-jacketed man now approaching the platform. "Ladies and gentlemen, please welcome Maestro Dieter Volkov."

Polite applause rippled across the room as the distinguished-looking man joined Carrie on the platform. He was tall and lean, his dark hair streaked with silver. One glance at his chiseled jawline and my assignment to be his dinner companion didn't seem quite so burdensome, after all.

"It is my great pleasure to be here." His European accent flowed rich and melodious over the crowd. "I look forward to making beautiful music with you all."

If Carrie hadn't clued me in that he was Russian, I'd have had trouble identifying his native country from his accent alone. But then, I hadn't traveled much. Not as much as I would have liked to. In any case, he sounded well educated and spoke fluent English. Probably some other languages, too—Europeans were often more diligent about learning multiple languages than Americans. And according to Carrie, he'd only been in the States a brief time. *I must ask him about his adventurous escape from Russia. Surely, he has a fascinating story to tell.*

And just like that, I couldn't wait to hear him tell it.

Chapter Three

After a few more remarks to the audience, Carrie again thanked the dashing musician, and he descended the platform. Moments after Michael Tate finished praying for the meal, the maestro pulled out the empty chair next to mine.

"Good evening." I extended my hand, hoping my palm wasn't sweaty. "I'm Amanda Parrish."

He turned to me with a dazzling smile. "Dieter Volkov. Pleased to make your acquaintance." As he took my hand in his, the calluses on the tips of his long, slender fingers, the result of countless hours, days, years spent practicing his instrument brushed my skin.

He released my hand, then sat. His profile looked strong and aristocratic in the flickering lantern light. "You are very kind to allow me to share your table, Mrs. Parrish."

"Oh, it's miss," I blurted, a little too hastily. My cheeks grew warm. Would he think I was signaling my availability? Nervousness accelerated my mouth into high gear, even as my brain pounded the brakes. "But really, Amanda is fine. We're not at all formal here at camp. And goodness, this isn't *my* table. Why, it's *everyone's* table. Here at Camp Harmony, we share and share alike. Don't we... everyone?"

A glance around the table showed each face staring as if I were spouting nonsense. Which, to be fair, I was.

Martha Barrington came to my rescue. "We're delighted you've joined us, maestro."

"It is Dieter, please." He threw a side glance in my direction. "Since we are being informal tonight." His mustache twitched. If I wasn't mistaken, he was suppressing a grin.

"My name is Martha Barrington, and this is my husband, Oscar. Oscar is an executive with the Goldwood Corporation," she added, as if Oscar were unable to speak for himself. After so many years of marriage to Martha, he'd probably given up.

One by one the rest of our tablemates introduced themselves. By the time the conversation circled back around to me, I had regained my composure and moved on to admiring the conductor's gracious manners. He looked to be around forty years old, give or take. Surely he'd had a noble upbringing, perhaps even been an aristocrat in his home country. What I knew about Russia wouldn't fill a thimble, but I could imagine him performing onstage in some ornate St. Petersburg concert hall, then escaping under cloak of night just before teeming hordes of armed marauders burst in and—

"Oh, maestro, you simply *must* tell us all about your adventures fleeing the riots!" Echoing my thoughts with uncanny precision, Martha leaned forward, a look of breathless anticipation on her flushed face. "How utterly thrilling that must have been."

Thrilling? Did she really say that running for his life must have been *thrilling*? My face burned with embarrassment at her gauche outburst. True, I was every bit as eager to pry into the gentleman's background, but I'd planned to pry with much more discretion.

A muscle tightened in Dieter's cheek. "Perhaps another time, madam. Tonight is about looking forward, not back."

"Carrie Tate tells me you took a tour of the camp earlier today," I ventured as the salad course was served, eager to change the subject.

"What do you think of our little music camp?"

"It is truly a marvel," Dieter said. "I'd read an article about it, but the scenery is much more breathtaking in person. I am most impressed by the facilities." He listed several things that he'd appreciated, including the spacious rehearsal hall and the smaller cabins used for lessons and practice. "And the biggest surprise was learning that the property is a hardworking logging camp throughout most of the year. Is that true?"

I nodded. "A highly productive one, too. You see, the Coker Lumber Company belonged to the family of Mrs. Tate's first husband. George Coker had always envisioned turning it into a music camp for young people. When Carrie inherited the property after his death, she was determined to fulfill his wishes. The logging takes place all fall, winter, and spring, but for six magical weeks during the summer—from around the middle of June to the end of July—Coker Lumber Company transforms into Camp Harmony."

Dieter's dark eyes shone. "Amazing. And Mrs. Tate, she accomplished this all by herself?"

"Goodness, no," Martha broke in. "That's the best part of the story. Mr. Michael Tate runs the bank in Timber Coulee, and he helped Carrie gather enough resources to both save the logging company and establish the camp. In fact, that's how they met. And now they've been married nearly as long as the camp's been in existence." She clapped her hands in glee. "Isn't it romantic?"

Martha was winding up like a gramophone. Thankfully, the serving of the main course interrupted before her conversational needle could drop too deeply into the Tates' personal affairs. Besides, it seemed awkward to discuss Coker Lumber Company's business in the presence of someone employed by its largest competitor, Goldwood Corporation.

Servers brought out steaming plates of roast chicken, and Dieter continued to share his favorable impressions of the camp.

"As I toured the grounds today, I was especially charmed by the beautiful flowers." In a wistful tone he added, "They remind me of the magnificent gardens of my homeland."

"Oh, do they?" Words failed me. *His homeland.* My heart melted in my chest. What must it have been like to flee one's strife-torn country with only the clothes on one's back? Although for all I knew, and by the looks of him, Dieter had sailed to America aboard a luxurious Cunard liner, with clothes not only on his back, but filling multiple steamer trunks.

He was a mystery, an enigma, and my curiosity flared again.

He took a sip of water, then said, "I'm an amateur gardener myself. I'm not very proficient at it yet, but I'm eager to learn. Do you keep a garden, Amanda?"

My name sounded almost lyrical, spoken in his mellifluous accent. I longed to hear him say it again. "I'm afraid not. I have quite the black thumb."

A look of confusion crossed his face. "A black thumb?" He glanced at my hands.

I stifled a giggle. "Here in America, when someone has a talent for gardening, we say he has a green thumb, because he can make plants grow and flourish. And someone who lacks a talent for gardening, such as myself, is said to have a black thumb, because we kill the poor, defenseless things."

"Ah. We have a murderess in our midst." The maestro and I shared a laugh, while the rest of the table looked on in bemusement. He cleared his throat. "I can see that the thumb of the camp's gardener is as green as can be. I should like to meet him sometime. Perhaps he can give me some, how do you say, pointers."

"I don't know who's responsible for the camp's flowers," I said. "But I'm sure Carrie Tate will be able to tell us."

"I'm pretty certain it was old Ernie Weiss," Martha broke in. "He's the camp handyman, doing carpentry work, repairs and such. But he's an avid gardener, too."

"That's right. That photograph in *Metronome* showed him tending the flower beds. Goodness, is there anything that man can't do?" I turned to Dieter. "You're in luck. I believe Mr. Weiss is working in the kitchen tonight. Would you like me to introduce you to him?"

He lifted a hand in protest. "Oh, no, not this evening. I would not want to interrupt the man in his work. I am sure he and I will have many opportunities throughout the summer to chat about hydrangeas."

Even the taciturn Oscar Barrington was moved to ask a question. "Which railroad brought you out here, the Northern Pacific or the Great Northern?"

As Dieter described his train journey from the Midwest, I sat back, content to listen. In spite of my initial reservations, he was proving to be both charming and witty. He filled his water glass from a pitcher on the table, the movement of his hands graceful and precise. A true violinist's hands.

Over dessert and coffee, he swung the conversation my way. "Have you always lived in Timber Coulee, Amanda?"

"Oh, dear me, no," Martha interjected before I could answer. "Our Miss Parrish is a city girl."

Dieter looked at me with fresh interest. "Is that so?"

"I'm afraid so, yes," I admitted, mildly perturbed at Martha. My former city-girl status often seemed to stand in the way of my being fully accepted by some Timber Coulee folks, even after ten years.

"Which city?" Dieter asked.

"Chicago."

"Chicago!" He sounded impressed, as if I'd named someplace exotic like Tokyo or Timbuktu, instead of the stockyards capital of the world.

"Have you been there?" I asked.

"I have not yet had the pleasure, other than to change trains." His dark eyes danced. "But I hear it is a marvelous city. How did it happen that you are here and not there?"

"A blizzard happened." I set down my dessert spoon. "I'd recently finished my studies at the American Conservatory of Music and was on my way to Seattle to accept a teaching position when the train I was riding got stuck in a snowdrift. I was stranded in Timber Coulee, and somehow I never left."

His smile was tender. "You sound like a woman who fell in love."

My stomach did a little flip. "I suppose I did. With the town, with the mountains, with the people... It's so beautiful and peaceful here. I don't ever think I could live in a big city again."

"And now you own a store? I believe that is what Mrs. Tate told me earlier, when she suggested we be dinner partners."

And thank heaven she did. "Yes. The Mountain Melodies Music Shop." If the name sounded silly to the sophisticated musician, he didn't let on. "We sell musical instruments and accessories, sheet music, Victrola records ... just about anything a musician could want. And I rent out the back of the shop to local musicians for lessons and rehearsal space."

"I will remember you when it comes time to replace a broken string." His grin was infectious. "And I will pray that one breaks sooner rather than later."

So will I. Surely my beaming face told him as much.

"These musical instruments you sell," he continued. "Are they new or used?"

"Both," I said. "Although we do have a lovely secondhand store in town, called Elite Repeat. You should visit it while you're in town, if you get the chance. Lots of local color."

I was about to explain that Heidi usually passed musical instruments on for me to sell because of my expertise, but just then Carrie tapped him on the shoulder.

"I'm sorry to interrupt, maestro, but it's time for you to play." She threw an eager glance at the rest of us seated around the table. "Mr. Volkov has graciously agreed to bless us with a sample of his talent."

Dieter stood and bowed to the table. "If you all will excuse me." Then to me he murmured "Perhaps we can continue our conversation later."

My insides did another flip. "I'd like that."

He strode to the platform and accepted a violin from one of the local musicians who'd been supplying dinner music. Then he lifted it to his chin and nodded to the accompanist. The sound that poured forth from the instrument was so enchanting, I could scarcely breathe. "Habanera" from *Carmen*, by Bizet. Never had I heard such a passionate and exquisite rendition of this familiar aria. How was it possible that I'd been sitting here, dining at Camp Harmony, with a man who could make his violin sing as though it were a human voice? A man so gracious and intriguing?

When he had finished, applause broke out around me, and I rose with the others. The smile he gave me when our eyes met made my insides melt like April snow on Mount Baldy.

"Bravo!" someone called out.

With a nod of acknowledgement to all of us, Dieter descended the platform and was immediately surrounded by a swarm of guests.

I caught Carrie's eye and gave her the thumbs-up signal. She glowed.

As the evening drew to a close, I turned to Martha. "Isn't he masterful? The camp is so fortunate to have him."

"He seems charming, and he certainly has talent." Her tone held a note of reserve.

"Martha." I lowered my voice. "Did you and Oscar receive that anonymous letter about Stuart von Bauer?"

Her face was a mask. "We did."

"I suppose the letter-writer is satisfied now that Mr. Volkov has replaced Mr. von Bauer."

"One hopes so," Martha said. "But I daresay we should have tried harder in the first place to procure an American."

The words hit me like a physical blow. "What do you mean?"

"Oscar and I feel the board made an error. After all, is our government not telling us to distrust any German, out of concern for our country's safety?"

"Oh, Martha, not you too. And Mr. Volkov isn't even German—he's Russian."

She locked her eyes on mine. "Don't be naïve, Amanda. Foreign is foreign. Who knows what kind of influence he'll have on the young people?"

I couldn't have been more astonished if she'd begun speaking Swahili.

"Oscar and I have discussed it," she continued. "We'll welcome him now that he's here. But next year, we'll find a nice, red-blooded American conductor."

I stood there, Scripture verses about welcoming strangers dancing on my tongue. But the steel in Martha's voice told me arguing would be useless. A more troubling thought crept in— could the Barringtons themselves have sent that anonymous letter to the board they served on? After hearing Martha's views, it no longer seemed impossible.

I was still fuming inside when James appeared to drive me home.

"Ready to go?" He caught sight of my expression. "What's the matter?"

"It's not important." It *was* important, vitally so, but in the moment, I didn't have the words to explain it all to James. "I think I'm just getting tired."

"You sure?"

My hand touched his sleeve. "Would you mind waiting here a moment? I want to pop into the kitchen and talk to Ernie. Mr. Volkov mentioned wanting to meet him, because of the flowers."

"Flowers?" James's forehead wrinkled in confusion.

"Yes. I'll explain later. Back in a minute."

I pushed through the swinging door to the kitchen. "Ernie, can you come here and—"

Sharp voices raised in argument stopped me in my tracks. Ernie and the cook stood facing each other in front of the stove. I couldn't make out the words, but from my vantage point, Dinah was mightily upset about something, waving her arms, and Ernie was returning as good as he got.

I lingered uncertainly for a moment, then retreated. This was not the time to introduce Ernie to our distinguished guest conductor. They'd have to talk about tulips at another time.

I returned to James and slipped my arm through his. "Let's go."

But all the way down the dark mountain, I thought about people I knew, people like Martha and Oscar Barrington and even old Ernie, and how different they could be on the inside from how they appeared on the outside.

When we reached town, the familiar Main Street shops blurred past, but they seemed different now, shadowed by fear and suspicion. Henderson's Hardware Store—was Mr. Schmidt still welcome to shop there? The church—would Reverend Miller cancel the German-language service? The high school—would German classes be removed from the curriculum?

What dark, ominous cloud had descended over Timber Coulee?

Chapter Four

The following Monday, before opening Mountain Melodies for the day, I hurried down the street to Elite Repeat. The ice wagon clattered past, making its morning deliveries, the horse's hooves thudding on the packed dirt of Main Street, while behind it a Model T honked its horn, the driver hollering with impatience.

Elite Repeat was a secondhand shop run by Heidi Fischer, a blond, pink-cheeked widow with an ever-present twinkle in her eye. A few minutes spent in Heidi's presence never failed to brighten my day.

The door swung open before I touched it. A tall, dark-suited older man emerged from the shop.

"Michael Tate! What a pleasant surprise."

"Good morning." He seemed to be taken aback by my presence.

"I've been meaning to congratulate you and Carrie on the success of the banquet. I had such a good—"

"Please forgive me, Amanda. I'm terribly late." He touched the brim of his hat and hurried down the street toward the bank. Startled, I stared at his retreating back. Normally, Michael was a friendly, jovial sort of fellow. But this morning, it appeared he had a bee in his bonnet. Or rather, his derby.

I shrugged it off and entered the shop, a pleasant jumble of old clothes, vintage china, antique furniture, decorative objects, and general flimflam. Elite Repeat was a delightful place to idle away a spare hour or two, if one had them, which I didn't.

"Heidi?" I called out, weaving my way past tables laden with bric-a-brac.

"In the back." Heidi's voice floated out from behind a heavy velvet curtain. "Just sorting through a new donation. I'll be right out."

I examined a delightful hat adorned with silk flowers until Heidi emerged, her arms full of linens.

"Say, I just ran into Michael Tate and—"

Her appearance halted my inquisition. Her usually rosy cheeks were pale, and there were dark smudges under her eyes that even her warm smile couldn't quite camouflage.

"Goodness, Heidi." I frowned, all inquisitiveness about Michael forgotten. "You look like you've been up all night wrestling with the ghosts of fashion past. Is everything all right?"

She dropped the linens on the counter with a soft thud. "Oh, you know me, always burning the candle at both ends. These vintage treasures won't sort themselves."

Her cheerful act didn't fool me for a moment. "Heidi Fischer, I've known you for as long as I've lived in Timber Coulee. What's really going on?" When she didn't reply, I pressed on. "I'm going to ask you something. And feel free to tell me that it's none of my business."

She looked dubious. "Now you've got me curious. What is it?"

"Ernie Weiss told me he's being harassed by that slick real-estate man, Leon Danvers. And he happened to mention that Danvers has been bothering you, too. Is that true?"

Her shoulders slumped. "He wants both our properties. Let's just say he's been ... persistent." She spoke barely above a whisper.

"Persistent?" A spark of anger ignited in my chest. "You mean he's harassing you about selling your house?"

Heidi nodded, smoothing a wrinkle from one of the linen napkins. "He came by again yesterday, waving blueprints for some new hotel. Said it would 'revitalize the neighborhood' and 'bring Timber Coulee into the modern age.'" She rolled her eyes. "As if we're all just dying to trade our homes for some soulless monstrosity."

I snorted, picturing Leon's idea of progress—one of those modern skyscrapers that belonged in a big city, completely out of character with Timber Coulee's sweet, small-town charm. "Well, if that's the modern age, I'd rather stay firmly planted in the past, thank you very much. Did you tell him what he could do with his blueprints?"

A ghost of a smile flitted across Heidi's face. "Not in so many words. I am a lady, after all."

"More's the pity. If I weren't a Christian woman, I'd have been tempted to give him an earful that would make his fancy Eastern investors blush."

Heidi's smile faded, and she glanced at the door. "He's not taking no for an answer, Amanda. Yesterday he … he implied that things might start getting difficult for me if I don't 'see reason,' as he put it."

A chill ran through me despite the warm summer air drifting in through an open window. "Heidi, that sounds an awful lot like a threat. Have you spoken to Sheriff Holcomb about it?"

She shook her head, twisting her hands in the folds of her skirt. "I don't want to make a fuss. Maybe if I just ignore what happened, Danvers will give up and move on to some other project."

"Or maybe he'll keep pushing until he gets what he wants." I reached out to squeeze her hand. "Heidi, you can't let him bully you like this. It's your *home*, after all."

Heidi's eyes welled with tears. "I know, but I'm scared, Amanda. What if he—"

The cheerful tinkle of the bell interrupted her, and we both turned to see Mildred Abernathy, the town gossip, bustling in, her hat askew and her cheeks flushed with excitement.

Heidi grabbed my arm. "Please don't say anything. To anybody."

"I won't."

"Heidi Fischer!" Mrs. Abernathy exclaimed. "You'll never guess what I overheard last night at Ernie Weiss's place." She saw me and stopped. "Oh, hello, Miss Parrish. I didn't see you."

"Good morning, Mrs. Abernathy."

"I suppose you're busy getting the music shop ready for camp season," the woman continued. "Busy time of year for you, and you left to run the shop all by yourself." She clucked her tongue. "It's a wonder you have time to stand around chitchatting with the neighbors."

I shot up a quick prayer for patience. "Thank you for your concern. I'm pleased to report I won't be all alone for long. My niece, Molly Mulroney, is coming for a visit. She's agreed to help me in the shop this summer, on her break from school."

"Well, I'm glad to hear it. That Callan MacTavish really left you in the lurch when he took off to go overseas." Mrs. Abernathy made it sound as if my former business partner had joined a leisurely Cook's tour of the British Isles instead of the Canadian military. "And leaving behind a wife and baby, too." Her lips flattened with disapproval. "That's what happens when people's loyalties lie elsewhere."

As if Callan's decision needed defending, I blurted, "Well, he *is* Scottish, you know. As a Scot, he felt a sense of duty to help Great Britain with the war effort. His father still lives there. And Rose readily agreed to it, so ..."

Even this was more information about Callan's personal affairs than I felt comfortable discussing. Time for a conversational pivot. "What were you saying about Ernie Weiss?"

Mrs. Abernathy hesitated. "Well, I'm not one to gossip," she began, untruthfully, "But I thought Mrs. Fischer might want to know, since she lives in our neighborhood."

"Know what?" A note of impatience colored Heidi's tone.

The woman's eyes glittered as if she were delighted to share a delicious tidbit. "Well. Late last night, I was out walking my little dog, Fifi, and I heard arguing as I passed Ernie's house. *Loud* arguing."

I turned to Heidi. "Did you hear anything?" After all, she did live right next door, and likely her windows would have been open to catch the summer breeze. Maybe she'd been lying awake, too, worrying about Leon Danvers's remarks.

"Not a thing," Heidi said. "But I might have been listening to the Victrola at that time. I do that sometimes when I can't sleep."

"You do play your music pretty loudly," Mrs. Abernathy commented. "I've been meaning to talk to you about that."

"What was the argument about?" Concern etched a line between Heidi's brows.

"I don't know," Mrs. Abernathy said. "I couldn't make out the words. But they sure sounded angry. Raised voices upset my sweet Fifi, so naturally, I didn't linger to listen."

Naturally. "Who was Ernie arguing with?" I pressed.

"I didn't recognize the voice." For someone so eager to share information, Mrs. Abernathy was irritatingly short on details.

A mental image popped up of the heated discussion I'd witnessed between Ernie and the camp cook. "Was it a female voice?"

"No, it was definitely a man. He sounded kind of tough, like one of those villains in the vaudeville shows." Mrs. Abernathy turned to Heidi. "I thought you'd want to know, so you'd be sure to lock your doors."

The specter of Leon Danvers floated to my mind, and probably to Heidi's, too. Danvers had moved to Timber Coulee from New

Jersey and spoke in a manner that, I supposed, could sound harsh to someone like Mrs. Abernathy.

Heidi remained quiet, but her wide blue eyes spoke volumes. High time to change the subject.

"I'm sure she will. Thank you, Mrs. Abernathy. And speaking of Molly," I said, harkening back to our earlier conversation, "I'd like to pick up a few things for her room. I've been using it for storage, you know, and I've cleared it out, but it needs a few homelike touches to make her stay more comfortable. I have in mind a clock for her bedside table and maybe something pretty to hang on the wall."

"I think I can help you out. Be right with you, Mrs. Abernathy." Heidi led the way to a ticking display of clocks of all shapes and sizes as Mrs. Abernathy busied herself with a rack of dresses. "Here you go. They all work. I've tested them." *Thank you*, she mouthed silently as she stepped away.

I examined the clocks, delighted to find a small brass alarm clock with a merry jangle. I had no clue whether my niece was an early riser, like myself, or preferred to sleep in—one of many things about her I looked forward to discovering.

Heidi returned with a couple of framed prints. "One of these should do nicely," she said, holding up the first one, a print of wispy Renoir ballerinas.

"That one's pretty, but—Oh, look," I exclaimed when I saw the second print. "This one shows Dorothy and her friends walking down the Yellow Brick Road. You know, from *The Wonderful Wizard of Oz*? That's always been Molly's favorite book. It's perfect—I'll take it!"

Heidi wrapped up my purchases. "Anything else for you today?"

"I don't think so, But, Heidi—"

With a glance at Mrs. Abernathy, I lowered my voice. "If there's anything I can do for you... anything at all..."

Heidi pressed my forearm. "I will let you know. I promise." She lifted her head and called out, "All right, Mrs. Abernathy, what can I help you with today?"

As Mrs. Abernathy launched into a dialogue about the declining quality of garments these days, I slipped out of Elite Repeat, the bright sunshine a stark contrast to the worry gnawing at my insides. An Eastern transplant, Leon Danvers had never been a very popular character around Timber Coulee, but making veiled threats to innocent people was going too far. As I unlocked the door to Mountain Melodies, I knew one thing for certain—I wasn't about to let him destroy my friend's life without a fight.

***

On Tuesday, I stopped in at Mrs. Wasserman's bakery on the way to meet Molly's train, remembering that my niece had a particular fondness for almond crescents. The welcoming scents of fresh bread and sweet pastries enticed me into the warmth of the bakery, but even so, something felt off. I glanced around, my gaze landing on the boarded-up window.

"Mrs. Wasserman?" I tried to keep the worry out of my voice.

The plump, gray-haired woman emerged from the back, her usually rosy face looking strained. "Good morning, Amanda. Your box of cookies is ready."

"Thank you, but ... what happened to the window?" I gestured toward the boards.

Mrs. Wasserman released a heavy sigh. "Someone threw a brick through it last night. Third time this month something like this has happened."

I gasped. "That's terrible! Have you called the sheriff?" Practically every conversation I'd had over the last few days seemed to involve urging people to call the sheriff.

She gave a bitter laugh. "Oh, I've reported it. But no one seems too concerned about protecting a German-owned business these days."

My mind scrambled in confusion. That didn't sound like James. "Because of what's happening over in Europe? What does that have to do with us?"

"Don't put your head in the sand, Amanda," Mrs. Wasserman's voice was voice low and serious. "Haven't you heard about the internment camps?"

My cheeks heated. "Well, yes, but ... those are for spies, aren't they? Spies and criminals." What had James had told me about the purpose of the camps?

She spoke with strained patience. "It's not just spies, dear. Ordinary citizens are being detained simply for being German. And it's not only Germans—all foreigners are under suspicion by some people."

Martha Barrington's comments about Dieter Volkov echoed in my head. "But that's ... that's terrible. How can they do that?"

"Fear makes people do ugly things." Mrs. Wasserman's gaze turned distant. "We've seen it before, and we're seeing it again."

As I paid for the cookies, my mind was reeling. How could this be happening in our town, in our country? The idea of Mrs. Wasserman—who'd been baking the best strudel in Timber Coulee for as long as anyone could remember—being seen as a threat was absurd.

"Is there anything I can do to help?"

She gave me a small, grateful smile and handed over the box tied with twine. "Just keep coming by, dear. And maybe ... maybe tell your friends that not all Germans are the enemy."

"I will. I promise."

I left the bakery, the weight of the cookie box in my hands insignificant compared to the weight of this new knowledge. The world seemed a lot more complicated than I'd realized.

My step lightened, however, as I strolled through Timber Coulee's modest train station, scanning the crowd for a familiar face. The anticipation of seeing Molly played an upbeat tempo in my heart.

"Choo-choo, Mama! Look." A voice pulled me from my thoughts.

My friend Rose MacTavish corralled her toddler, who was imitating a locomotive, complete with arm-wheels chugging along. The wife of my former business partner, Callan, and a talented violin teacher herself, Rose had traded her teaching career for motherhood when little Emil was born.

"Ahoy, there, little engineer!" I took a seat next to Rose. "And how is my favorite mama today?"

Rose's smile was warm enough to melt butter on a hot biscuit. "Armed with snacks, ready for battle." Her eyes twinkled as she hoisted her son onto her lap. "My sister's returning from Montana today. She's been helping her sister-in-law, who just had a baby."

"Any news from Callan?"

"He's doing well, keeping spirits high and letters flowing. He says he's got enough yarns to knit us a new house." Rose's smile waned. "But I'm afraid I have some less cheerful news... Have you heard?"

"Heard what?" The shift in her tone caused concern. I leaned in, instinctively grasping her free hand.

"Oh, Amanda." Tears trembled on the ends of Rose's lashes. "Ernie Weiss is dead."

Chapter Five

"Ernie's dead?" A wave of despair crashed over me. "But how is that possible? He seemed perfectly healthy. Fit as a fiddle, in fact. I just saw him the other day. He fixed that old piano for me." I paused for breath, wishing that were my last memory of him, that I could erase the troubling sight of his heated argument with the camp cook. "What happened?"

"I ran into the sheriff on the way here." Rose's words were muted by the rushing in my ears. "He gave me the news and told me Carrie Tate had telephoned him yesterday from the camp. She'd gotten worried when Ernie didn't show up for work and asked the sheriff to check on him."

A vision of Ernie lying alone brought tears to my throat. *Think, Amanda.* "Do they know what happened?"

"A freak accident, James said. Apparently, he tumbled down a flight of stairs and broke his neck."

A crack split my heart. "Oh, no. Poor Ernie."

Rose's expression mirrored my shock. "It's a real shame."

"Such a sweet man." The words seemed inadequate, but in the moment, they were all that came to mind. "Have they notified his next of kin?"

"What next of kin?" A tear trickled down Rose's cheek. "The man lived all alone for who knows how many years. What do we really know about his background? I've never heard him speak of a family, have you?"

"No," I said. "But he always had such a happy demeanor. I guess you never really know a person, what they're going through."

"Indeed." Rose squeezed my hand before releasing it as the ringing bells and distant rumble of the approaching train signaled the change of subject.

"Speaking of family, it looks like our reunions are right on schedule." Leaving the cookie box on the seat, I stood and brushed away the melancholy with a determined smile. Devastated as I was over Ernie's tragic and unexpected demise, I determined not to let anything spoil my happy reunion with my niece. Life in Timber Coulee always had a way of blending the bitter notes into its sweet melody.

The train chugged into the station with a cheerful huff, and Rose and I scanned the crowd as passengers disembarked in a bustle of activity. Soon Rose was reunited with her sister. As they strolled off with little Emil between them, I craned my neck to spot a head of familiar brown curls among the crowd, my tummy fluttering in anticipation.

"Aunt Amanda! Over here!" Molly's voice cut through the clamor, brightening my spirits. My niece bounded toward me, violin case in hand, and I held out my arms to embrace her.

"Molly, darling! You're all grown up and city-fied. Let me look at you." I stepped back, keeping my hands on Molly's shoulders. Her dark curls were bobbed fashionably short, sure to fuel endless debate at Maxine's Beauty Parlor. "What a lovely young woman you've turned out to be! How many years has it been since we've seen each other?"

"Too many. Say, how do you like my new glad rags?" Molly laughed, stepping back to twirl in her smart travel ensemble with a startlingly short hemline—barely covering her calves! My own trusty blue cardigan and long skirt felt frumpy by comparison. "Mother and I splurged at Marshall Field. 'You must make a proper impression on the folks in Timber Coulee,' she said. I promised her I wouldn't look too fresh-from-the-farm."

"Sounds like something my sister would say. Well, once Timber Coulee gets a look at you, it won't know what hit it. How are your parents, by the way?"

"Oh, fine. They send you their love."

I picked up the box of cookies and linked my other arm through hers. "Now, let's collect your luggage, then go home and get you settled."

As we strolled down Main Street, I had to admit that her shorter skirt was practical for navigating our dusty streets. I pointed out various landmarks with a flair that could rival any seasoned tour guide. "And that's the Majestic Theater, where your auntie once played a duet with a magician's rabbit—don't ask. Over there's the hotel. At four stories, it's the tallest building in town." *Unless Leon Danvers and the New Century Development Corporation have their way.* I pushed the unwelcome thought out of my mind just as quickly as it popped in.

Molly made enthusiastic comments as I prattled on, as if taking it all in. "Timber Coulee seems to be full of character—and characters."

"Both in abundance," I agreed. "That steeple over there is the church I attend. And next to it is the new bookstore, run by Mrs. Swanson. She's got a whole section dedicated to local authors. We have exactly two." I slowed our pace to a stop. "And here we have the pièce de résistance, our humble shop."

Molly set down her suitcase and violin on the sidewalk and rubbed her arms. Her eyes sparkled as she read the sign above the door. "Mountain Melodies Music Shop. Oh, it looks just as I imagined, the way you described it in your letters."

"We'll come back tomorrow after we've gotten you settled at home. I've closed the shop for the day, in honor of your arrival."

Molly looked perplexed. "But won't you miss out on business? Isn't there anyone to mind the store for you when you can't be there?"

"Not since Callan MacTavish left. That's one reason I'm so pleased you were able to come and help during our busiest season. But not the only reason, nor even the most important one." I slid an arm around her slim shoulders. "The most important reason is that I get to spend time with my favorite niece."

"Your *only* niece," she reminded me with a nudge to the ribs.

"*And* my favorite. Now that you're all grown up, I just know we're going to be good friends. Come on, my house is right around the corner." She picked up her bags, and we continued on our way. "Now, tell me how you've been. Timber Coulee must feel like a world away from Chicago."

"It does. And even farther from Mother and Dad's farm in Indiana." Molly kicked a pebble along the sidewalk. "I'm grateful for a time away from both. It's nice to have a change of scenery, you know?"

"I do know," I said. "And for my part, I'm grateful for your help in the shop during this busy season. Your timing is impeccable."

"Happy to lend a hand—or an ear. And maybe sneak in some practice time. I need to keep my skills sharp for next semester at the conservatory or I might lose my place."

"Ah, I sense a competitive spirit," I nudged her. "The true mark of a Parrish woman."

"Or a Mulroney one," Molly countered with mock seriousness, eliciting a warm laughter that echoed between us. Having lived on my own for so long, I'd forgotten how good it felt to be in the presence of family.

We approached my sunny yellow cottage. As I'd told Dieter, I wasn't much of a gardener, but had made an extra effort on my house-guest's behalf, and was pleased to see the pansy beds were looking decent. We were about to climb the front steps when a familiar figure called to us from across the street. It was Sheriff Holcomb, his uniform crisp and hat tilted back, revealing a warm smile.

"Hello, James," I called.

He crossed the street. "Hello, Amanda. Good afternoon, miss." Looking with curiosity at Molly, he touched the brim of his hat.

I made the introductions. "James, I was so sorry to hear the news about Ernie. Rose MacTavish told me. That must have been awful for you to discover his body."

He grimaced. "All part of the job. The worst part, I'll admit."

Molly scanned my face. Her smile faltered. "A body? What happened?"

My excitement dimmed. My "welcome to Idaho" plan hadn't included sharing such sad news. "Sorry, Molly. A good friend of ours, Ernie Weiss, passed away, quite suddenly. I've only just learned about it myself, and Sheriff Holcomb here was the first on the scene."

"Oh, no. I'm sorry to hear that." Molly's face fell, her exuberance replaced by the solemnity of the news.

"A tragic accident. Isn't that right, James?" I added, not wanting the shadow of death to loom over our reunion.

"Looks that way," James said. "We'll know more once we've collected all the evidence. I'm on my way back to the house now to meet the team."

"Evidence? You mean it might *not* have been an accident?" Molly shivered.

"Of course it was an accident," I reassured her. "The sheriff is just being extra thorough. Isn't that right?" When James took too long to answer, I barreled on. "Ernie was an older man. It's quite possible he was more frail than he appeared, and took a nasty tumble down the stairs. But let's not dwell on it right now. I'll fill you in later. For now, let's get you settled. Good to see you, James."

James's gaze lingered on me for a moment before he tipped his hat again. "You two have a good day."

"You too, sheriff," Molly chimed in, her tone playful as she waved goodbye. But while her good mood was restored, mine was shadowed by nagging doubts. It just didn't seem possible that Ernie had fallen down the stairs by accident, and it seemed like James didn't think so, either. And yet, what other possibility could there be?

As we entered the front door, Molly turned to me with a sly smirk. "So, is Sheriff Holcomb somebody special?"

"What? No." I rolled my eyes, but I couldn't hide my amusement at the very idea.

"I'm just saying," Molly teased, "he was practically blushing when he talked to you."

"He's just being nice. He's always been like that, sort of bashful. We're good friends, that's all. His late wife, Sarah, sang with me in the ladies' choir."

"If you say so." Molly's grin widened. "But any fool can see he's definitely sweet on you."

I shook my head. "You're impossible."

She followed me upstairs to the guest room. The quaint space was barely large enough to fit a single bed and a small dresser, but it would have to do.

"Here we are, sweetie. I hope you'll be comfortable."

Molly stepped in, her brown eyes appraising the busy floral wallpaper and frilly curtains. "It's lovely, Aunt Amanda. Truly."

Something in her tone said otherwise. "Do you really like it?"

She turned and gave me a quick hug. "It's a cozy little nest, like you'd find in a storybook."

That had indeed been the effect I'd been aiming for. But it dawned on me that I'd prepared the room for the little curly-haired girl I remembered, not for the sophisticated young woman standing before me in a sleek, modern traveling coat and smartly tilted hat. Suddenly, the room seemed overly fussy, festooned with frills. And whatever had possessed me to prop my childhood teddy bear among the ruffled pillows?

"Tell you what. We can visit Elite Repeat, our local secondhand shop," I told her. "Get you some things more suited to your taste. Heidi always has the most interesting assortment of items." I pondered how to discreetly remove the Yellow Brick Road picture before she saw it and replace it with something more suitable.

"Oh, the room suits me fine the way it is," she insisted. But her look of relief was unmistakable.

I patted her arm. "We'll go this week. For now, why don't you wash up and then rest a bit? That train journey must have been exhausting. Are you hungry?"

"Not very. I ate a hearty breakfast on the train," she admitted. "A nap sounds very appealing. But are you sure we shouldn't go and open up the shop?"

"I'm sure. But will you be all right if I pop out for a while? Much as I hate to leave you alone the moment you got here, there's something I need to take care of."

"I'll be fine," she assured me. "I think I'll unpack my things and then grab forty winks. I won't even know you're gone."

Gently, I closed the door, then hurried downstairs and down the street toward Ernie's house. Since James and his team were going to be poking around, then I wanted to be there too, out of respect for my friend.

And to seek reassurance that his tragic death had, indeed, been an accident.

The neighborhood where Ernie lived lay on the east side of town, next to the railroad tracks. Identical to most others on the block, his house was a small, simple worker's cottage, with a front room and a kitchen on the first floor and two bedrooms on the second. The afternoon sun slanted across the living room as I stood in the doorway, my heart heavy with grief and growing suspicion. The musty scent of old books and furniture polish hung in the air, a familiar smell now tinged with something unsettling.

"I just can't believe it," I murmured to James. He stood beside me, his brow creased. "This isn't like Ernie at all."

James scanned the room. "I know what you mean. It's a right mess in here." He turned to me, his expression stern. "But as I told you, you shouldn't be here. Let me and my men do our job."

Ignoring him, I stepped carefully into the room, mindful of the clothes and papers strewn about. My foot caught on an overturned stack of books, sending them tumbling. As I bent to pick them up, my spine tingled with a sudden realization.

"James, Ernie was always so neat. Almost compulsively so. Remember how he used to joke that even his dust bunnies were organized? And he was meticulous about his tools." I swallowed past the lump in my throat, remembering the day he'd repaired my old piano. The last day we'd spent together.

A ghost of a smile flickered across James's face. "Yeah, I remember. He was mighty proud of the way he kept his old wagon in order."

I straightened up, clutching one of Ernie's books to my chest. "So why does it look like a tornado tore through here?" My fingers traced the faded fabric of a shabby upholstered chair. A well-used guitar leaned against it. "It's like he was interrupted," I mused. "And never came back to finish."

James stepped closer, his presence reassuring. "Amanda, I know you're hurting. We all are. But sometimes accidents just happen, even to the best of us."

I turned to face him, my resolve hardening. "An accident that leaves a meticulous man's house in complete disarray? And I told you how Mrs. Abernathy said she overheard someone shouting in Ernie's house the other night. Have you spoken to her yet?"

James rubbed the back of his neck. "You know how Mildred Abernathy can be. Always poking her nose where it doesn't belong, hearing things that might not be there."

"But what if she did hear something?" I moved further into the room. "Ernie wasn't one for raised voices." A brief memory concerning his argument with the camp cook flashed across my brain, but I pushed it away as being uncharacteristic of my friend. "You know that as well as I do. Don't you see? Something doesn't add up here."

He held my gaze for a long moment. "All right, Amanda. What are you thinking?"

I took a deep breath. "I'm thinking we need to look closer. Maybe ... maybe Ernie's death wasn't an accident at all."

James's eyebrows shot up. "I'll admit, I have my doubts, too. But murder, or even manslaughter, is a mighty serious accusation. Do you have any idea who might have wanted to harm Ernie?"

I bit my lip, thinking. "Well, there's Leon Danvers. He's been pressuring folks to sell their properties. Maybe Ernie refused and things got heated? And then there's ..." I paused.

"There's what?"

"I wasn't going to mention it, but remember on the night of the banquet, how I told you I was going to introduce Ernie to Dieter Volkov?"

"Yep. But you changed your mind."

"I changed my mind because when I went into the kitchen, Ernie was in the midst of a heated argument with the cook, Dinah. It looked pretty serious, so I left them to it."

"So you think Dinah might have wanted to do him harm, or something?"

I raised my hands in frustration. "Oh, I don't know." The theory did sound pretty preposterous, now that it had been spoken out loud. "But I sure wouldn't put it past Leon Danvers. Or maybe it's somehow connected to the anti-German faction. With a last name like Weiss ..." My unfinished thought lingered in the air.

"It's possible," James conceded. "But so far the vandals seem interested only in doing harm to property, not people. And we can't jump to conclusions and go around accusing people. We need evidence."

My mind was already racing. "Then let's find some. Will you help me look around? There might be something here we've overlooked."

"There is no *we* in this, Amanda. You should go home and let us do our jobs." James tried his best to sound stern, then—seeing I wasn't going anywhere—gave in. "All right, but we need to be careful. If this does turn out to be a crime scene, we don't want to contaminate any evidence. Here, put these on." He handed me a pair of thin gloves. "I'd rather you not leave fingerprints all over the place. Just in case."

"Of course." I moved toward the stairs. "We'll be careful. But, James, I can't shake this feeling. Ernie was hiding something, and I think whatever it was might have led to his death."

We continued to search, my heart pounding with a mix of anticipation and dread. What secrets had my old friend been keeping? And more important, had those secrets gotten him killed?

The bedroom was in similar disarray to the rooms downstairs, drawers opened and belongings strewn about. The tousled bed had clearly been slept in. Had Ernie been awakened from a sound sleep by a noise? A prowler, perhaps? Then, sleepy and disoriented, stumbled down the stairs to his death?

I picked up a framed photograph from Ernie's bedside table. It showed a solemn bride and groom from several decades past. To my surprise, the bridegroom was a much younger version of Ernie, arm in arm with a woman I'd never seen before. On the back, in faded ink, was written "Mr. and Mrs. Ernest Weiss, 1874."

"Oh, Ernie," I whispered, "What else don't I know about you?"

With renewed determination, I set the photo down and continued my search. Whatever the truth was, I was going to find it, For Ernie's sake.

And for the sake of justice.

Chapter Six

A couple of hours later, no more enlightened about Ernie's fate than when I'd started, I left James and his men at the task and made my way back home, not wanting to leave Molly on her own too long.

"Do you think it would be all right if I took his guitar?" I asked James.

"Not today. We might need it for evidence." His brown eyes held sympathy. "But I think he'd want you to have it. When we're done with it, I'll make sure you get it."

At home, still thinking of Ernie, I hummed one of his favorite hymns as I began preparations for supper. The gentle clanking of pots and pans filled the cottage with a homey atmosphere. It was nice to have somebody to cook for.

A thumping noise at the door interrupted my culinary efforts. I wiped my hands on my apron and went to answer it. Who could be calling at this hour? As I opened the door, I was greeted not by a person, but by a familiar meow. There, sitting on the doorstep with an expectant look on his face, was Moxie. Thanks to a small window in the stockroom left permanently open on his behalf, he came and went from the shop as he pleased.

"Well, hello there, you furry rascal. Decided to come in for supper, have you?"

Moxie meowed again, more insistent this time, and I stepped aside to let him in.

He sauntered past me, his tail held high like a flag, and made a beeline for his water bowl.

I closed the door and followed him. "You've got impeccable timing, as always." I returned to chopping vegetables for a refreshing salad while chicken soup simmered on the stove.

When he'd slaked his thirst, Moxie wound himself around my ankles, purring loudly. I came close to tripping over him as I moved between the counter and the stove.

"All right, all right." I reached down to scratch behind his ears. "I know what you want. Just let me finish this first."

I stirred the pot on the stove, the rich aroma of herbs and spices filling the air.

Moxie sat nearby, his green eyes following my every move.

When I opened a cupboard to fetch a can of tuna, his ears perked up.

"You're not fooling anyone with that innocent act." I spooned the fish into his bowl. "You're as much a glutton as you are a charmer."

Moxie meowed in what I could only interpret as agreement before diving into his meal. As I continued preparing supper, I chatted to him, telling him about Molly's arrival and the plans for her stay.

He purred and meowed at appropriate intervals, as if he understood every word.

"You'll have to be on your best behavior while we have a guest. No midnight concerts or bringing in 'presents' from the garden, understood?"

Moxie blinked at me slowly, which I chose to take as a promise. I checked the icebox and made a mental note to put out the card for extra ice tomorrow. Now that summer had arrived, things spoiled so quickly.

With a final stir of the soup and toss of the salad, I relished the sense of contentment that settled over me. The cottage felt alive with the fragrance of simmering onions, Moxie's contented purring, and the knowledge that Molly was resting nearby.

After a harrowing afternoon, it was shaping up to be a lovely evening indeed.

When Molly came downstairs, a purring presence wound between her ankles.

"Molly, meet Moxie." I'd mentioned him to her in one of my letters and hoped to high heaven she liked cats. I needn't have worried.

"Oh, what a darling kitty!" She scooped Moxie into her arms, and he butted his head against her chin, a sure sign of approval.

Over a fragrant supper of soup and salad, I regaled Molly with tales of Timber Coulee. Most of the stories seemed to involve old Ernie in one way or another, his various adventures and misadventures around town. The cottage rang with laughter, the sadness of loss tempered by the warmth of cherished memories.

At last, I carried our dishes to the sink and put a few of Mrs. Wasserman's cookies on a plate.

"So, are you excited about getting to see the music camp? I thought we'd ride up there on Sunday and have a look."

Molly's eyes lit up as she helped herself to an almond crescent. "Oh, absolutely! I can't wait to meet Stuart von Bauer. Your letters made him sound so impressive!"

Oops. Forgot that little detail. "Ah. About that … There's been a bit of a change. I'm afraid Stuart von Bauer won't be conducting, after all."

"Oh, no!" A shadow passed over her delicate features. "What happened?"

"Well, it seems Mr. von Bauer fell ill at the last minute," I explained. "But not to worry. They've found a wonderful replacement. A violinist named Dieter Volkov will be conducting the orchestra instead, and also teaching the strings program."

Molly's disappointment was evident. "Dieter who? I've never heard of him."

I leaned in with a conspiratorial air. "Now, don't look so glum. I've heard him play, and he's really quite remarkable. A Russian virtuoso, they say, with fingers that make magic on the strings."

"Is that so?" Molly perked up a bit. "Well, I suppose if you say he's good ..."

"Oh, he is," I assured her with a little more enthusiasm than I'd intended. A slight heat rose to my cheeks. In truth, I hoped to accidentally-on-purpose run into Dieter when I took Molly up to the camp.

Molly must have noticed my expression, because she raised a curious eyebrow. "Aunt Amanda, you seem quite taken with this Mr. Volkov."

I waved a dismissive hand. "Honestly, Molly. You've barely been in town ten minutes and you're already trying to pair me off. First Sheriff Holcomb, and now Dieter." I surprised myself by how easily I referred to him by his first name, a detail I could be sure my inquisitive niece did not miss. "I simply appreciate good music when I hear it. Now, speaking of music, I've also talked to Carrie Tate about the possibility of you playing with the camp orchestra in the grand finale concert. How would you like that?"

Molly's eyes widened. "Me? But I thought I was too old for camp."

"You are, officially. But, unofficially, they often invite local musicians of all ages to participate in the final concert, to round out all the parts and make a big impression on the audience. People will come from as far away as Spokane, you know, to hear the Camp Harmony grand finale concert. It's an annual rite of summer for music-lovers."

"I'd love to! But aren't you going to participate? Surely they can use your cello skills."

I shook my head. "My cello-playing days are over. But you, my dear, are a talented violinist, and playing with the orchestra will be a wonderful experience for you. It may even enhance your credentials back at the conservatory. I know the Tates would be delighted to have you."

"Really?" Molly's excitement was palpable. "You think they'd let me?"

"I don't see why not," I replied. "But the final decision will be up to the conductor. Why don't we talk it over with Carrie on Sunday? In fact, we'll bring your violin with us, in case you can play for Maestro Volkov then and there." I fervently hoped so. "Then rehearsals are set to begin the following week, two evenings a week."

Molly practically levitated. "Oh, Aunt Amanda, that would be amazing! But are you sure you don't mind not participating yourself?"

I reached across the table to pat her hand. "Not at all, sweetie. I'll be far too busy at Mountain Melodies. Besides, I'll get to attend the concert and cheer you on. That will be reward enough for me."

"You're the best!" Molly exclaimed.

A spirit of mischief shot through me. "Well, I do try. And who knows? Maybe we'll even have an adventure or two along the way."

***

Mountain Melodies's quaint wooden storefront, adorned with painted musical notes and a slightly weathered sign, welcomed a bustling crowd on the warm Saturday morning. While Camp Harmony was located several miles from Timber Coulee's business district, the re-purposed lumber wagon made the round-trip between camp and town several times throughout the day. bringing a steady stream of excited campers and staffers to the shop. Their animated chatter and occasional experimental plucks or toots added to the cheerful cacoph-ony filling the store.

At the counter, a line formed as camp counselors purchased sup-plies. Fresh strings for well-worn guitars. New drumsticks to replace those invariably lost or broken. Reams of sheet music for upcoming talent shows and sing-alongs. I offered advice and shared jokes as I rang up purchases. Moxie lounged in the sunny window display, keeping a lazy eye on our activities.

Whooshes of wind each time the door opened fluttered the sheet music and announced new arrivals every few minutes—a harried-looking music director rushing in for emergency valve oil, wide-eyed first-time campers clutching allowance money and eyeing candy-colored recorders, and local musicians stopping by to chat and check out the latest stock.

"Aunt Amanda," Molly said, "Where do you keep the violins? A customer is asking for one, but I didn't see any on display with the other stringed instruments, and I can't find any in the stockroom, either."

"I'm afraid we're clean out of violins at the moment," I told her. "I have a shipment on order, but they haven't arrived yet. See if you can interest the customer in a viola instead." I was only half joking. Violas were the most underrated instruments in most orchestras, in my opinion, and could use a little boosting now and then.

Watching Molly in action was a delight, her bobbed curls bouncing above her shoulders and her white-stockinged ankles peeking out from under her fashionably short hem. She'd picked up the details of clerking in the store with brisk efficiency, from how to run the cash register to where the extra stock was kept. Not that any of it was especially difficult, but there were a lot of little procedures to remember. I was grateful to have her capable assistance and that she was able to get up to speed without too much delay.

"You're a natural," I praised. Her eyes sparkled with pride.

Now, with three days' experience under her belt, she grew more confident with each interaction as customers flowed in and out. Her cheerful laughter was a stark contrast to Mrs. Abernathy's sharp intake of breath.

"Good heavens." Disdain pinched the older woman's nostrils. "Miss Parrish, is that your niece? Why, she looks positively... modern."

I put on my friendly-shopkeeper face. "Have you come for the Chopin? Molly, do you have a moment to help Mrs. Abernathy with her sheet music?"

Molly seemed oblivious to Mrs. Abernathy's scandalized expression. "Of course! What can I help you find? We just got in some fascinating new jazz pieces from New Orleans. They're all the rage in the cities, you know."

Mrs. Abernathy's face puckered as if she'd bitten into a sour lemon. "Jazz? My word. No, thank you. I'll stick with Chopin, if you please."

"Oh, but you simply must give it a try," Molly insisted, her eyes sparkling with enthusiasm. "It's so lively and expressive. I've even been learning some of the dances. Perhaps we could organize a social at the town hall to introduce—"

"Molly," I interrupted gently, observing Mrs. Abernathy's reddening face. "Why don't you fetch that Chopin nocturne from the back room?"

As Molly disappeared behind the curtain, the scent of her rosewater cologne lingering in the air, Mrs. Abernathy leaned in close. "Really, Miss Parrish," she whispered, her breath smelling of cloves, "You ought to keep that girl in check. What with her outlandish clothes and talk of wild dancing... why, she'll be wanting to run for mayor next!"

"Oh, I wouldn't worry too much, Mrs. Abernathy. Molly's just full of youthful enthusiasm. Now, about that sheet music..."

Mrs. Abernathy's face took on its trademark I've-got-a-tidbit gleam, and she leaned even closer. "I was just lunching with Martha Barrington at the hotel restaurant, and guess who we saw there."

"I can't imagine." Few things interested me less.

"Heidi Fischer and Michael Tate. Lunching together. Alone. Just the two of them."

"Fancy that," I droned. I knew what she was implying, but refused to give her the satisfaction of thinking I believed the situation was anything but above-board. After all, they were in a crowded restaurant, in the middle of town, in the middle of the day. Nothing suspicious about that. "Heidi's a customer of the bank. Perhaps they were having a business discussion."

"They had their heads together, speaking quietly," Mrs. Abernathy said, likely annoyed that they weren't barking their business in voices loud enough for her to eavesdrop on the conversation. "What I think, and Martha agrees with me, is that—"

Mercifully, her spurious speculation was interrupted by Molly returning with the Chopin nocturne. As I completed Mrs. Abernathy's transaction, I wondered how many more feathers Molly's modern ways would ruffle in our little town, and felt a mischievous rush of pleasure that they'd ruffled Mrs. Abernathy's.

But I also couldn't help the unwelcome vision that edged into my mind—that of Michael Tate leaving Heidi's shop so early the other morning. I could scarcely believe that anything the slightest bit inappropriate could be taking place between two such upstanding people.

But that was the trouble with gossip. It planted seeds where no seeds should be planted and then caused them to take root and flourish.

By early afternoon, the crowd had subsided. I glanced at the wall clock. "It's just about time for me to leave for Ernie's funeral," I said to Molly. "Are you sure you'll be all right on your own for an hour or two?"

"Sure thing." Her eyes held sympathy as she put her hand on my shoulder. "I know this is a difficult day for you. Take all the time you need."

I patted her hand, thankful that I didn't need to close the shop on such a busy day, but could leave it in her capable hands. Then I walked down the street to the church.

The sanctuary was filled. Ernie had touched so many lives. I nodded a greeting to a few familiar faces, then slid into a pew next to James, who'd saved me a seat. Michael and Carrie Tate sat a few rows ahead of us. After Mrs. Abernathy's absurd implications, the sight of them sitting side by side in their usual pew was comforting and reassuring. Though I didn't have a clear view from my vantage point, knowing the Tates, I was pretty sure they'd be holding hands. I sat back, satisfied that Mrs. Abernathy was just a meddling gossip.

I listened, my eyes stinging but dry, as the pastor's eulogy for Ernie washed over me. The air felt heavy with grief, punctuated only by a few muffled sobs and the occasional rustle of clothing. As I tried to focus on the words being spoken, a persistent sniffling caught my attention.

Turning my head, I spotted Dinah, the camp cook, seated across the aisle, a few rows behind us. Her round face was crumpled in sorrow, shoulders shaking as she dabbed at her eyes with a sodden handkerchief. While we were all saddened by Ernie's death, the intensity of her grief was surprising.

Later, as we gathered in the church basement for the reception, I approached Carrie, who was arranging a platter of sandwiches. The mood had lightened somewhat, but Dinah's anguish still weighed on my mind.

"Carrie," I murmured, "I couldn't help but notice how upset Dinah seems. Is she okay?"

Carrie glanced over to where Dinah sat alone in a corner, still dabbing at her eyes. "Thanks for mentioning it. I should check on her."

Before she could walk away, I touched her arm. "Carrie, there's something else I've been meaning to ask you. Did you... did you receive a copy of that anonymous letter?"

Carrie's expression hardened for a moment before she forced a smile. "Oh, that? It's nothing to worry about. Just the work of some crank trying to stir up trouble. We get things like that from time to time."

"I see." I didn't, really, but hesitated to harp on the issue. "Are you sure? Because it sounded like the Barringtons—"

"I am sure," Carrie said firmly. "Now, let's see to Dinah."

She made her way to Dinah's table. I trailed behind, then hung back as she sat beside the distraught cook and placed a comforting hand on her arm. "Dinah, honey, what's troubling you so?" Carrie asked in a soothing tone.

Dinah looked up, her face a mask of misery. "Oh, Mrs. Tate," she choked out, "I feel just awful. That night, at the patron's banquet..." She trailed off, overcome by a fresh wave of tears.

"What about the banquet, Dinah?" Carrie prompted.

I eavesdropped without shame as Dinah drew a shuddering breath and launched an explanation. "The stove was acting up something fierce. I was so stressed, trying to get everything cooked on time. When

Ernie offered to help, he got in my way, and I... I snapped at him." Her voice dropped to a whisper. "I said such terrible things. And now... now I'll never get to apologize."

My heart ached for Dinah, for the pain evident in her voice.

"Oh, Dinah," Carrie soothed, "Ernie knew you didn't mean it. He understood how stressful your job can be."

"But those were the last words I ever said to him," Dinah sobbed. "How can I live with myself?"

Carrie squeezed Dinah's hand. "Jesus forgives you, Dinah. And I'm certain Ernie did too. He knew your heart."

"You really think so?" A glimmer of hope appeared in Dinah's tear-filled eyes.

"I know so," Carrie affirmed. "Would you like to pray together?"

Dinah nodded. Carrie bowed her head and asked the Lord for comfort and forgiveness. I joined her in silence, deeply moved by the scene unfolding before me. Warmth spread through my chest as Dinah's grief begin to lift—a poignant reminder that even in our darkest moments, faith and forgiveness could bring light.

Despite my own sorrow, a profound sense of gratitude rushed through me for the compassion and healing I'd just witnessed. It was a bittersweet comfort, knowing that Ernie, a devout Christian, was in the presence of Jesus. And even in his absence, his spirit of kindness would live on in the way we cared for one another here in Timber Coulee.

I crossed Dinah's name off my mental list of people who might have wanted to harm Ernie. But the question remained. If it wasn't Dinah, then who—if anyone—was it?

Just then, a gentle touch landed on my shoulder. James stood beside me, his eyes filled with concern.

"Hey. How are you holding up?"

"I'm... managing. It's all still so difficult to comprehend."

James's hand moved to my back in a comforting gesture. "I know. Listen, Amanda, if you need anything—anything at all—you let me know. All right?"

His sincerity struck a note deep inside. "Thank you, James. That means a lot. I only wish that we'd found something in his house that would have—"

"Amanda." His voice was firmer now. "Let it go."

I exhaled. "You're right." Nothing to be gained by wondering. Time to admit defeat.

Maybe.

As we stood there in companionable silence, a complex mix of emotions washed over me. Grief for Ernie, concern about the mysterious letter Carrie had dismissed, gratitude for James's support, and a lingering unease about the circumstances surrounding Ernie's death. A small part of me couldn't shake the feeling that there was more to his death than met the eye—a mystery that I was somehow meant to unravel.

Despite my sorrow, despite James's appeal to move on, a renewed determination rose to uncover the truth, whatever it might be.

Chapter Seven

On Sunday after church, Molly and I stopped home for a quick bite to eat before our planned visit to Camp Harmony.

"Ready for a bit of an excursion?" I wrung out the dishrag after our simple repast.

Molly hung the towel on the peg. "I just need to pop upstairs and grab my violin. I haven't touched it since I've been here, but I've been so busy getting acclimated."

"You've only been here a few days. You'll catch up."

"Yes, but what if Mr. Volkov wants me to play for him right away? I'm afraid my playing won't be up to par."

"Relax," I assured her. "He'll understand you've been traveling. And, after all, this is Camp Harmony, not Carnegie Hall."

I hoped my words were true, both that she would play well and that Dieter would find her skill level sufficient for his orchestra.

While she trotted upstairs, I finished putting away the dishes, wiped the counter, and checked Moxie's food supply. I was still in the kitchen, filling His Majesty's water bowl, when an anguished cry came from Molly's room. My heart leapt into my throat as I rushed up the stairs.

"Molly? What's wrong?"

She was kneeling on the floor, her violin case open before her, cradling the instrument in her trembling hands. Even from where I stood, I could see the ugly crack running along its body.

"It's broken." Her voice was thick with unshed tears. "It must have happened on the train from Chicago. I... I didn't even think to check it on Tuesday when I arrived. If I'd been practicing all along, as I should have been, I would have seen it the moment I opened the case. But we've been so busy in the shop, and I've had so much to learn and so many people to meet, and—" The dam broke and a flood of tears halted her speech.

I knelt beside her and placed a comforting hand on her shoulder. "Oh, Molly. I'm so sorry."

She looked up at me, her eyes wide with panic. "What am I going to do, Aunt Amanda? What will I practice on? If I can't practice, I'll lose my place at the conservatory. And the Camp Harmony orchestra... I can't play with them without a decent instrument!"

She broke into sobs as the reality of the situation crashed over her. Molly's violin wasn't just an instrument. It was her ticket to a better future, her chance to escape the life she'd left behind on the farm in Indiana. I couldn't bear to see her dreams crumbling before my eyes.

"Now, now." I tried to keep my voice calm and reassuring. "Let's not get ahead of ourselves. We'll figure this out."

Molly shook her head, her voice rising. "But how? Mountain Melodies doesn't have any violins in stock. You said so yourself, re- member?"

She was right. Darn that slow shipment! Then an idea struck me.

"Molly, listen to me." I lifted the broken violin from her hands and set it aside. "We'll talk to Rose MacTavish. She's a good friend of mine, a violin teacher who's taking a break from teaching while raising her little boy. Chances are good that she'll have a violin you can use."

"Do you think so?" Molly sniffled.

I squeezed her hand. "What are friends for? I'll go right over to the shop and telephone her." I didn't yet have a telephone at the house, though installing one increasingly seemed like a good idea. "And if she doesn't have one, maybe the camp has an extra one you can use."

Molly threw her arms around me, nearly knocking me over. "Oh, Aunt Amanda, thank you! You're a lifesaver!"

As I hugged her back, a swell of pride mixed with my concern. It felt good to be able to help, to have the means to make a difference in someone's life.

"Now," I said, pulling back and wiping a stray tear from her cheek, "let's get a cup of tea and then we'll take a look at your violin. Maybe it's not as bad as it looks."

She sniffled again. "But aren't we going up to the camp this afternoon?"

Setting aside my own disappointment not to see Dieter, I squeezed her shoulders. "Why don't we put that off for another day? I think you've been through enough. And once we get Rose's violin, you can practice on it so that you're comfortable when you audition for Mr. Volkov. Now, why don't you go and put the kettle on while I run out and make that phone call?"

We rose, and Molly cast a last, mournful look at her broken instrument. "Do you really think it can be fixed?"

"I'm sure of it. As soon as possible, we'll take it to Floyd Hendricks over in Spokane. If anyone can repair it, he can."

Molly's shoulders relaxed a little at that. On the way to the store to use the telephone, I silently hoped that my optimism wasn't misplaced. Something told me that Molly's violin—and by extension, her future—now rested in my hands.

Alas, Rose wasn't available. Her sister informed me she'd taken Emil for a visit to his grandmother and wouldn't be back for a couple of days. So, bright and early the next morning, Molly and I paid a visit to Elite Repeat. The scent of lavender and old books greeted us, along with Heidi's cheerful voice from behind a mountain of pasteboard boxes.

"Amanda! Just the lady I wanted to see." Heidi called out, her bright curls bouncing as she popped up from behind the counter. "And you must be Molly. Welcome to Timber Coulee, dear."

"Thank you." A good night's sleep seemed to have restored Molly's good humor after the previous day's tragedy.

After a brief exchange of pleasantries, I said, "Heidi, I don't suppose you have any violins on hand."

"I'm afraid not," Heidi said. "And if I did, I'd have handed it over to you. I always do, when it comes to musical instruments."

"I thought so. You're very kind to keep me in mind. Just thought I'd ask." I briefly explained about Molly's broken violin. "I'm completely out of stock, and we're hoping to find a replacement soon so she can play in the camp orchestra."

"I'm so sorry, dear," Heidi told Molly. "I promise if I do receive one, you'll be the first to know. In the meantime, come have a look at these treasures." Heidi gestured to the boxes. "Poor Ernie's belongings. Since he had no family, the sheriff's asked me to handle the disposition of his worldly goods. I've just begun sorting through them, and the sheriff tells me there's more to come. All the proceeds from the sale of Ernie's things will be earmarked for a special scholarship fund for Camp Harmony." Sorrow filled her expression. "I still can't believe he's gone, can you? Such a sweet man. I miss him so much."

I patted her arm, my throat too constricted to speak.

"And now Leon Danvers will be able to scoop up Ernie's property and tear down his house," she added, bitterness lacing her tone. "Soon I'll be living in the shadow of a skyscraper."

"You don't know that," I soothed. "Let's wait and see how it all plays out. There's a Chamber of Commerce meeting tomorrow. Perhaps I should bring it up there."

Heidi looked horrified. "Leon's a member of the chamber."

"Exactly," I said. "The chamber forbids its members to engage in shady business practices. Maybe they'll pressure him to stop."

"Please don't, Amanda. I don't want to get the chamber involved. It will only anger Leon. Although, it wouldn't surprise me if Leon kicked Ernie down the stairs himself, just to get his hands on that property," Heidi growled.

"Oh, Heidi, you don't mean that." Her blunt accusation startled me, even though privately I'd been thinking along those lines as well. "Leon Danvers may be a shady character, but I can't believe he'd go that far."

Or would he?

I glanced at Molly to see if she'd heard our conversation, but she was staring at the tower of boxes, her eyes wide.

"Goodness, that's a lot of stuff for one person."

"You'd be surprised what people accumulate over a lifetime," Heidi said with a wink. She hefted a box onto the counter.

I peered into the box and felt a surge of delight at its contents. "Oh, my! Is that a collection of books?"

"Indeed, it is." Heidi nodded. "There are scads of them. Ernie must have been quite a reader."

Molly reached into the box. "Look at these old volumes." She ran her finger along the spines. "Ooh. *The Adventures of Huckleberry Finn.* I've always wanted to read that! And look at this adorable photograph!"

She picked up a seashell frame holding a small, sepia-toned photograph.

"Well, what do we have here?" The image showed two young men in their late teens or early twenties, one blond and one darker, arms slung around each other's shoulders, mugging for the camera in front of an elaborate fountain. They were dressed in the height of 1890s fashion, complete with straw boater hats.

"Aren't they good-looking?" Molly leaned in for a closer look. "They look like they're having a grand time. I wonder who they are."

I slid the photo from the frame and flipped it over. In faded ink, someone had written: "Luke and Bobby, World's Columbian Exposition, Chicago, 1893."

"The World's Fair," I murmured. "Can you imagine how exciting that must have been for these boys?"

Something poked at my brain as I studied the face of the young man labeled "Luke." There was something oddly familiar about him, but I couldn't quite place it. Someone I'd known back in my Chicago days, perhaps?

"Heidi," I said, "Did Ernie ever mention anyone named Luke? or Bobby?"

Heidi shook her head. "Not that I recall. Why do you ask?"

"Oh, no reason. It's just . . . this Luke fellow. I could swear I've seen him somewhere before."

"A long-lost sweetheart, perhaps?" Molly giggled. "Someone you met at the conservatory when you were a student, back in the dark ages?"

I gave my niece a playful swat. "Don't be silly. This picture is over twenty years old. I would have been—let's see—only around twelve years old when it was taken. So, no. Besides," I added with a hint of wistfulness, "I think I'd remember if I'd met a young man that good-looking."

"In any case, I think I'd like to buy that seashell frame," Molly told

Heidi. "It'd look adorable in my room. But I don't need the photo."

"I think I'd like to keep it. Heidi, would you mind?"

"Not at all," she replied.

I slipped the photo into the pocket of my skirt, hoping I'd remember to take it out before wash day. Molly paid for her purchase, then we scurried to open Mountain Melodies for the day. But all morning long, I couldn't shake the nagging feeling that the face in the photograph was important somehow.

In the middle of the afternoon, the shop telephone rang.

"Sheriff Holcomb on the line," the operator's nasal twang informed me.

"Amanda? I'm wondering if you'd have time today to pop over to Ernie's. There's something I think you should see."

"Can it wait?" I asked. "I'm kind of tied up here."

"Well, it's not an emergency, but we are trying to clear out the rest of Ernie's things by the end of the day. Since he had no next of kin, the county's eager to empty the house and put it up for sale."

"So Leon Danvers will be able to snap it up?" I couldn't keep the sneer out of my voice.

James hesitated. "I suppose so. At least, he'll have as much chance to place a bid as anyone else."

That wasn't what I wanted to hear. "So New Century will be able to build their hideous skyscraper, after all." *We must make room for progress, Amanda.*

"Not yet. Not if they don't get Heidi Fischer and the other affected homeowners to sell as well. They can't erect a building that size on Ernie's lot alone." I heard the note of optimism in his voice and grabbed onto it for dear life.

"I see." *Deep breath.* So there was a chance to save Timber Coulee from a monstrosity, as long as Heidi could hold up against whatever pressure Leon Danvers could dish out.

"Almost everything from Ernie's place has been going to Elite Repeat, household goods and such," James explained.

"Yes, I know. Molly and I were in there just this morning. Heidi told us about the scholarship fund, too." A bright spot in an otherwise dismal situation. The photograph came to mind. "James, do the names Bobby or Luke mean anything to you, in connection with Ernie?"

"No. Who are they?"

"No matter," I said. "Just something we found at Heidi's. I'll show you later."

"Anyway," James continued, "We found some stuff I thought you might want to take a look at first, before we hand it over to Heidi."

Curious about what he wanted to show me, I left Molly in charge of the shop and hurried over to Ernie's place. The rooms were largely empty now, but James led me into a dusty shed set well back on the property, tucked within a small cluster of trees, right next to the railroad tracks. Inside, the air was thick with the scent of old wood and forgotten memories.

"To be honest, we almost missed it, hidden back here in the woods," James admitted. "There's not much here, just a few random tools and things, but there's a pile of stuff I think you'll find interesting." He gestured to a stack of wooden fruit crates teetering in the corner. "Why Ernie stored it in this old shed, I guess we'll never know."

"These crates don't contain farm-fresh produce, then, I take it." What could they hold? "More evidence of Ernie's... shall we say, haphazard lifestyle."

The word "raw" was scrawled in faded ink across the side of each dirt-smudged crate. "Raw, huh? As supposed to dried or preserved, I suppose." The clusters of grapes painted on the side of one crate, a selection of apples on another, looked appetizing, and my stomach rumbled. That's what I got for skipping lunch.

James sneezed as he used a claw hammer to pry the lid off a dust-covered crate. "Turns out old Ernie had quite the collection of musical instruments, records, sheet music. All the junk you like."

"Did he?" Now he had my attention. "And it's not 'junk,' by the way. It's memorabilia."

"Whatever you say."

Sifting through the contents, I puzzled over Ernie's connection to all this. He loved music, and a guitar sang under his touch, but he was more of an American-folk-tunes kind of fellow, judging by the types of Victrola records he purchased in my shop. The materials in this box all seemed related to classical, orchestral music. What was he doing with all this ... memorabilia?

Another thought nagged at me. If Ernie didn't want these items, why hadn't he handed them over to me to sell on his behalf? It seemed unlike him to keep them hidden away like this, like buried treasure in a pirate's lair.

"Wonder where all this came from," I said, more to myself than to James. "It doesn't seem like Ernie's usual taste. Do you think someone might have given it to him?"

James shrugged. "Could be. Ernie had a lot of friends over the years. Maybe he was holding onto it for someone."

The mystery of it all intrigued me. There was a story behind these boxes, one that Ernie had taken with him.

After a quarter-hour of looking, I straightened and stretched my spine. "This is all fascinating, James, but I really do have to get back to the store. I'd love to take a closer look. How much longer will the crates be here?"

"We want to clear everything out today, but I can drop all this off at Mountain Melodies, if you'd like." James's voice held a touch of kindness, as if he sensed my emotions were on edge. "I'll bring them by tomorrow."

"That'd be great. I have a Chamber of Commerce meeting in the afternoon, but the morning will be fine."

Part of me wished I could ask Ernie about the history of these musical treasures, to understand why he'd kept them hidden away all these years. But perhaps some mysteries were meant to remain unsolved, a silent melody echoing through time.

Chapter Eight

"Thank you, sir. Come back and visit us again."

As the customer left Mountain Melodies, he held the door open for James, who was maneuvering through the entrance, his arms laden with a dusty crate.

"Special delivery." The door slammed behind him. "Courtesy of our late friend Ernie Weiss."

My pleasure at seeing my friend and excitement over the musical treasures he'd brought me was tempered by a wave of melancholy.

"Oh, Ernie." My friend would have relished the adventure of ferreting through a box of mysterious items. Something he'd never get to do again. And even worse, this time he was the source of the mystery.

James set the box on the counter. Moxie jumped up and sniffed it with supercilious feline curiosity.

"Well, hello there, Moxie." James scratched him behind the ears. The cat rewarded him with a loud purr, arching into his touch.

"He misses Ernie too, I think. He always brought him little treats when he came by the shop." My eyes filled with unexpected moisture.

"Are you all right?" James's voice was soft with concern.

I managed a watery smile. "I will be. It's just... seeing his things here in my shop, it makes it all feel so final, you know? Ernie was such a fixture in town. It's hard to believe he's really gone."

"Yeah, I know." James cleared his throat. "I've got several more crates out in the Dodge. Where do you want them?"

"Let's put them in the stock room. It'll take me a while to go through them, and I don't want them cluttering up the sales floor. I'll take this one." I hoisted the wooden box.

"Careful you don't get a splinter. These crates are pretty beat up." James's protective gaze lingered on me a moment longer than usual. Probably figured I'd shrivel like a delicate rosebud the moment he turned his back.

"Got it." I wasn't the rosebud type, and he knew it.

"I'll go get the rest."

Molly closed the cash register and followed me into the stockroom. "What's all this?"

"James brought us some treasures from Ernie's house. Want to help me unpack?"

"Sure!" She eyed the crate with curiosity. "Did he work in a grocery store?"

"Not that I'm aware of," I said. "He may have, at one time. Who knows? He'd lived a long life even before I met him. More likely he just grabbed these good, sturdy boxes that a store was throwing away." Looking at them, my mind started churning with possibilities. After a good sanding and a coat of paint, they'd be handy for displaying books or plants. But first, we had to empty them.

Molly and I unpacked the crates as James lugged them in, discovering a treasure trove of musical items. Dusty gramophone records, a tuning fork, and even a few small instruments—a clarinet, a piccolo—emerged. Moxie hopped onto a nearby shelf and supervised the situation with interest.

"Oh, look. Here's a souvenir program from the Chicago World's Fair. It says, 'A concert of the Chicago Symphony Orchestra, featuring violinist Imogene Lansdorf.'" I showed the accompanying photograph to Molly. "Would you look at that hat? Is that a bird sitting on it?"

"I'll bet it was the pinnacle of fashion in 1893." We shared a laugh, then Molly said "Ooh."

"More surprises?"

"Yes." She dipped into another crate, dug out a sheaf of musical scores, and handed them to me.

"Oh, look at this." I flipped through the yellowed pages. "Bach, Beethoven... lots of German composers. I don't think our more... patriotic neighbors would appreciate these much." I'd meant the remark as a joke, but it didn't seem the least bit funny.

James, hauling in the last crate, raised an eyebrow. "No, I suppose not. It's a shame, really. Music should transcend borders."

"These are fantastic!" Molly said. "I can't wait to play some of these pieces." From the front door, the bell signaled a customer's arrival. "I'll get that." She dusted her hands on her smock and hurried out to the sales floor.

"Perhaps I should offer these scores to Dieter." I set them aside. "They might be useful to him at the camp."

Something flickered in James's eyes. Was it annoyance? "Ah, yes, the great Dieter." His tone was laced with sarcasm. "Didn't realize the two of you were on a first-name basis already."

What was his problem, all of a sudden? "We got fairly well acquainted at the banquet, and it seemed silly to stick to—oh, never mind." Realizing I'd hit a nerve, I changed the subject. I didn't owe him an explanation, anyway.

I looked at the stack of sheet music. "Our anonymous letter writer would have a fit if he or she saw this. You'd think all German music was a personal affront to some people."

James stepped back and rubbed his forehead, a weary expression crossing his face. "Yeah, some folks are getting a bit... hot under the collar about anything German these days."

"More trouble?"

"Another incident at the bakery. And there's been a lot of talk. In fact, the government's sending an agent, a fellow called Callaway, to give us a hand. Supposedly he specializes in these sorts of investigations of situations that could possibly affect national security."

"Oh, dear. That sounds serious."

"It is serious."

I touched the top sheet of yellowed paper, my fingers trailing over its worn surface. Moxie rubbed against my arm, offering comfort. "It's so unfair. As if the music itself is somehow tainted just because of where it came from. Ernie would have hated that kind of thinking."

"I know. It's a shame people can't see past their prejudices." James held up a hand. "I have something else for you. Wait here."

"Where am I going to go?"

He returned in a minute, carrying Ernie's guitar and a battered notebook. My throat tightened as he handed them to me.

"I sold Ernie this guitar," I said. "Years ago, but I remember as if it were yesterday. And this notebook... all his songs..."

"I saw the way you looked at them the other day," James said. "I'm sure Ernie would have wanted you to have them."

"Thank you, James." I caught a whiff of bay rum, a subtle, woodsy scent, and became acutely aware of how close we were standing. "Well." I took a step back. "I suppose I'd better get to work sorting through all this. Thank you for bringing it by, James. The cartons and the guitar. It means a lot to have a piece of Ernie here."

"My pleasure. Maybe I'll stop by later to see how you're getting on. And, Amanda... if you need to talk about Ernie, or anything else, I'm here."

His intimate tone flustered me. Maybe Ernie's death hit him harder than he wanted to admit. "Thanks, James." I squeezed his arm in a sisterly fashion. "You're a good friend, you know that?"

A flicker of—of what? disappointment?— crossed his face, but disappeared as quickly as it appeared. The moment was broken by a horn honking outside.

"Oh, that'll be Tommy getting impatient." James forced a smile. "I should get back to work."

As he turned to leave, he gave Moxie one last pat. "Keep an eye on her, will you?" he murmured to the cat, who mewed in response.

I walked with him to the front of the store. "James?" He turned, his hand on the doorknob, a look of hope in his eyes. "Thank you for this. For everything. You're like family to us."

His gave a stiff nod. "Anytime, Amanda. That's what friends are for, right?"

As the door closed behind him, I leaned against the counter, feeling a twinge of guilt. For what, I didn't know.

Molly bid farewell to the customer, then gave me a curious look. "Is everything okay?"

"Fine." I returned to the stockroom with a sigh and ran my hand over the sheet music. "Oh, Ernie," I whispered, "I hope you know how much you meant to all of us."

Moxie nudged my hand with a soft purr. I scratched under his chin. "You're right, Moxie. He knew. And we'll make sure his music lives on." Then, squaring my shoulders, I set to work, determined to honor my old friend's memory through the music he'd left behind.

***

Focusing on work proved difficult as the conversation with James, both about Ernie and about the bigoted attitudes of some people in our town, disrupted my concentration. The more I thought about the poison-pen letter and the harassment of people perceived as foreign, the hotter my blood boiled.

The Chamber of Commerce meeting would provide a good distraction. Here was a chance to discuss the issue face to face with fellow business owners and figure out how we could put an end to it. For once, maybe the normally perfunctory gathering would provide a useful outcome.

The hot, cramped back room of the First National Bank smelled of coffee, cigar smoke, and Judith Hensley's generous application of *Quelques Fleurs*. Stanley Cooper, president of the Timber Coulee Chamber of Commerce, rapped his knuckles against the oak table, calling the meeting to order. Twenty faces turned toward him, our usual jovial pre-meeting chatter falling silent.

"Friends." Stanley's voice carried the weight of seventeen years as owner of Stan's Barber Shop. "I'm sure you've all heard about what happened at Wasserman's Bakery last night."

"Sheriff Holcomb mentioned it to me," I said, "but I didn't get the details."

"Someone painted a nasty slogan across the front window," Judith said. "And she'd just had that window replaced, too, after someone hurled a rock through it."

A murmur rippled through the gathered business owners. David Henderson, who ran the hardware store two doors down from the bakery, slapped his palm on the table. "Bunch of cowards, that's what they are. Coming in the dead of night to break windows and paint that... that filth."

"Has anyone seen Mrs. Wasserman today?" asked Betty Collins

from the flower shop. "I tried to stop by this morning, but the shop was closed."

"She's staying with her sister in Mill Creek," Judith replied. "Sheriff Holcomb is investigating, but..." She let the sentence hang, and everyone understood its meaning. Small-town law enforcement had its limitations, especially when it came to matters like this.

Frank Moore, the town's only insurance agent, shuffled through some papers. "I've already started the claim paperwork, but with the new exclusions regarding civil unrest..." He adjusted his wire-rimmed glasses. "Well, it's complicated."

"Complicated?" Ted O'Reilly stood up so quickly his chair scraped against the floor. The owner of O'Reilly's Pub gripped the back of his chair, knuckles white. "There's nothing complicated about it. My family came here with nothing but the clothes on our backs, and people called us all sorts of names. Said we were papists and worse. But Mrs. Wasserman? She's as American as any of us. In fact, her boys are volunteering overseas to help the Allied cause."

"Both of them," added Miss Pierce, the librarian. "Jimmy's serving with the Canadian forces in England, and David's driving an ambulance in Europe. She showed me their letters just last week."

"Has anybody looked into the Liberty League?" Judith asked. "They're always blowing hot air about keeping Timber Coulee American. Maybe they're causing this trouble."

"Now, hold on a minute." Oscar Barrington raised his voice a notch. "Several of us here are also members of the Liberty League, and we resent your implication. We're all businessmen here. And ladies," he added with a grudging glance at me. "We all only want what's best for our town."

Several voices murmured agreement.

Michael Tate, who'd been silent until now, pushed his ledger forward. As the bank's manager, his words carried weight. "The fact is, whether the insurance covers it or not, we can't let this stand. This isn't just about Mrs. Wasserman's window. It's about who we are as a community."

"That's exactly what I think," I said. "We need to decide what we're going to do about it."

"Do about it?" Leon Danvers scoffed from his corner, his gaudy plaid vest straining across his rotund midsection. "What can we do? Times are tough. None of us has extra to spare."

"Maybe not individually," said Rachel Green. The milliner's fingers twisted in her lap. "But together? I have five dollars I can contribute right now."

"Ten from me," Ted O'Reilly said quickly, pulling his wallet from the pocket of his waistcoat.

"Now, hold on." Leon raised his hand. "Where does it stop? If we start helping every time something happens—"

"Every time?" Stanley Cooper's voice cut through the room like steel. "In thirty years, can you name one other time we've needed to help a member of this chamber rebuild after vandalism? One other time when someone's business was attacked simply because of their family name?"

Leon's mouth opened, then closed.

Judith pulled out a small tin box from her purse. "I'm putting in fifteen dollars. Who's next?"

One by one, they came forward. Some could only spare a dollar or two, others gave more. Even Leon Danvers eventually shuffled up with a crumpled five-dollar bill.

"We're at ninety-eight dollars," Judith announced after counting. "That should cover the window and the paint removal."

"Make it an even hundred," Miss Pierce said, reaching for her coin purse.

"The money's important," Betty Collins spoke up, "but what about preventing this from happening again? We need to take a stand."

"Agreed," Stanley said. "I propose we draft a statement from the Chamber condemning these acts of vandalism and affirming our support for all our business owners, regardless of their heritage."

"Put it in the Timber Coulee *Gazette*," Miss Pierce suggested. "Right on the front page."

"And we should take turns keeping watch at night," added David Henderson. "I can see the bakery from my upstairs window. I'll take first shift."

"I'll help," Ted O'Reilly volunteered. "The pub's open late anyway."

Judith looked around the room. "All in favor of these measures, raise your hand."

The vote was unanimous.

"Before we adjourn," Stanley Cooper said, "there is one other matter we need to discuss. I've received the final proposal from New Century Development Corporation about their new hotel."

My ears perked up. The energy in the room shifted immediately. This had been a topic of heated debate for weeks.

"Six stories?" Herbert Wilson's voice cracked with disbelief. "It'll cast a shadow over the whole downtown."

"It'll also bring in lots of new jobs," countered Oscar Barrington. "And those workers will need to eat lunch somewhere, shop somewhere, live somewhere."

"You would say that, Oscar," Ted O'Reilly said. "I hear Goldwood's been investing heavily in the project."

"It'll be good for Timber Coulee." Oscar shrugged. "A rising tide floats all boats."

"Good for Goldwood, you mean," Ted grumbled. "Lots of lumber goes into a building that size."

I saw my chance and seized it. "Mr. Danvers, I'm surprised New Century wants to put a luxury hotel smack up against the railroad tracks. Won't guests' slumber be disturbed?"

Leon's plump cheeks colored crimson. "If you knew anything about hotel development, Miss Parrish, you'd know that proximity to the railroad station is paramount for the traveler's convenience."

"Proximity to the station, yes, but why not somewhere further away from the tracks? Like that field on the western edge of town that's currently uninhabited. A hotel built on that spot would still be within walking distance of the station, yet not displace any residences. And it would be situated on the... the more attractive side of town." I was about to say *swankier*, but no place in Timber Coulee could really be called swanky.

"New Century has conducted thorough market studies, and they've determined the east side of town is the place to put it." Leon folded his arms.

"It's also nearer the Goldwood plant," Oscar interjected, "making it a convenient place to house our visiting executives and clients."

"But not convenient at all for the homeowners who would be displaced." I pressed on. "Some of us have been hearing interesting stories about how New Century's been securing the property."

Leon, who'd been lounging against the back wall, stepped forward. "I'm not sure what you're implying, Amanda, but New Century's land acquisitions have been completely above board." His smile never quite reached his eyes.

"Really?" I heard the steel in my voice. "So you haven't been paying late-night visits to homeowners? Telling them their properties will be condemned anyway, so they might as well sell now?"

"I don't know what you're talking about." Leon spread his hands in a gesture of innocence. "Every sale has been properly documented and freely negotiated."

My fingers tightened on the arms of my chair. I could still hear Heidi's voice describing how Leon had shown up at nine o'clock at night, talking about eminent domain and inevitable property devaluation. But I'd promised her I wouldn't repeat her story without permission.

"Let's keep to the facts at hand," Stanley interjected, clearly sensing the tension. "The proposal before us is about zoning approval, not individual property transactions."

Betty Collins shook her head. "But what about our town character? We're a warm, friendly place. No one wants to see a modern monster looming over the courthouse."

"Times change," Stanley said. "Maybe they need to."

Ted O'Reilly leaned forward. "What about a compromise? Could we ask them to scale it down? Maybe four stories instead of six?"

"We've already compromised," Leon growled. "You may recall that the original plan was for twelve stories."

I scanned the faces around the table. The same people who'd just united so decisively over Mrs. Wasserman's window were now clearly divided. Progress versus preservation—it was an old battle in Timber Coulee.

"We don't need to decide today," Stanley said. "But we should schedule a special meeting soon to vote on this. Everyone should have time to review the new proposal and talk to their neighbors about it. And now, let's take a ten-minute recess before tackling the next item on the agenda."

Nearly everyone stood, some to stretch their muscles, some to refill their coffee cups.

"Need some fresh air," Oscar said to no one in particular. He headed for the door, then turned and jerked his head as a signal for Leon to accompany him. What were those two up to?

I followed at a discreet distance until they turned down the alley. I couldn't follow them there undetected. There they huddled, speaking too quietly for me to hear what they were saying. But they'd unwittingly planted themselves next to an exhaust vent, and it occurred to me that the old bank building's pipes and vents had always carried sounds in strange ways. I'd been startled on previous occasions by hearing disembodied voices floating up through the radiator in the ladies' room, but this time it might work in my favor.

Back inside, made a beeline for the ladies' room. Judith was standing in front of the mirror, dusting powder over her nose. I waited in a stall until she left, then came out and knelt beside the radiator. Sure enough, voices drifted clearly through the pipes.

"Leon, we need those properties." The gravelly tone belonged to Oscar. "The site is perfect for our project, and Simon won't take no for an answer."

Who was Simon? Someone at New Century? At Goldwood?

"I'm telling you, Oscar, these people are stubborn." Leon's usually smooth voice sounded strained. "They're not interested in selling, no matter what I offer."

"Listen here." Oscar's voice dropped lower, but the vent carried every word. "I don't care what it takes. Use that silver tongue of yours. If that doesn't work, well...accidents happen, don't they? Rickety old houses can be so dangerous."

"Amanda, what are you doing? Are you all right?"

I hadn't heard Betty enter the room.

"Fine, fine, just adjusting my stockings." My hands trembled as I straightened and smoothed my skirt, the implications of the overheard conversation sinking in. First the pressure tactics with Ernie and Heidi, and now this? My mind raced to Mrs. Wasserman's vandalized bakery. Could these two be behind the vandalism incidents, using the anti-foreigner angle as a ruse? These two were active members of the Liberty League, after all, an organization known to be hostile toward foreigners under the banner of being patriotic. How many "accidents" would Timber Coulee endure before someone spoke up?

"I've been meaning to ask a favor of you," Betty said. "The Mountain Meadowlarks have been talking."

"Have they?" I was only listening with half an ear. The other half was still straining to hear Oscar and Leon, but the radiator had gone silent.

"We've been trying to think of something special we could do to honor Ernie's memory."

I gave up on espionage and turned to Betty. "Who is?"

She tilted her head. "The Meadowlarks."

"Ah." The community ladies' choir met twice a month to rehearse in the back room of my shop. "How sweet of you all. What did you come up with?"

"We'd like to learn one of Ernie's songs and sing it at our fall concert. We were hoping you'd arrange one of them in four-part harmony for us."

"What a thoughtful idea," I said. "I think I could do that. I have his songwriting notebook. It'll have to wait until August, though, after camp season ends. I won't have much free time between now and then."

"Oh, thank you," Betty breathed. "That's fine. We won't start rehearsing until after Labor Day. Well, I hear Stan rapping his gavel. I guess we should get back to the meeting."

I put her out of my mind the moment she left the room, and

tossed one more glance at the silent radiator. Then I checked my lipstick in the mirror more out of habit than vanity, and took three deep breaths. The face that looked back at me was pale but resolute. I couldn't unhear what I'd heard through the radiator, and I couldn't stay silent—not anymore. But I'd need to be smart about this. Careful. The sort of men who talked about orchestrating "accidents" weren't the sort to take kindly to interference.

Chapter Nine

When I got back to the shop, my voice trembled as I asked the operator to connect me to the sheriff's office. The conversation I'd overheard still echoed in my mind, making my stomach churn. James's familiar voice answered.

"Sheriff Holcomb speaking."

"It's Amanda." I lowered my voice, though I was alone in the shop. Molly was in the stockroom, ferreting through Ernie's crates. "I need to tell you something. It's about Leon and Oscar."

There was a pause on the other end. "Go on."

"I overheard them talking outside the Chamber of Commerce meeting today. They didn't know I could hear—I was, um, powdering my nose." I took a deep breath, trying to keep my voice steady. "They were discussing how to convince homeowners to sell their property to New Century. Oscar advised Leon to increase the pressure."

"Did he make any suggestions for doing so?" James's tone had shifted, becoming more clipped and professional.

"No, but James..." I hesitated. "The way they were talking—Oscar specifically said, 'Accidents happen.' And he said something about rickety houses being dangerous. I wrote it all down."

"I see." I could hear papers rustling in the background. "Amanda, listen to me carefully. This is exactly the kind of information we've been waiting for, but I need you to act completely normal around these two. Don't avoid them, don't watch them, just behave exactly as you always do."

"But shouldn't I try to—"

"No." James cut me off. "My department will handle this. We have protocols in place for exactly this type of situation. Getting involved could compromise our work and potentially put you at risk."

Frustrated, I twisted the telephone cord around my finger. "Are you sure? Because maybe they're also tied somehow to the vandalism around town. They certainly seem capable of it. I could maybe try to get more information—"

"Amanda. You've done exactly what you should by reporting this. But these men are powerful, and they're dangerous. If they suspect they've been compromised, they won't hesitate to protect themselves. Do you understand what I'm saying?"

I swallowed hard. "Yes. I understand."

"Good. Now, I'm going to have my team look into this immediately, but I need you to promise me something."

"What?"

"Promise me you'll stay out of it. No amateur detective work, no eavesdropping, no nothing. Can you do that?"

I thought of how close I was to the situation, how easy it would be to gather more information. But finally, I sighed. "I promise."

"Thank you. And Amanda? You did the right thing calling me."

After we hung up, I sat in the lengthening shadows, the receiver still warm in my hand. I couldn't shake the feeling that I'd just set something huge in motion—but whether I'd done enough, or too much, or too little, I couldn't tell.

***

Over several days, Molly and I continued to unpack Ernie's crates. We could only work at it sporadically, between serving customers and doing other shop-related tasks.

"We'll take our time," I told Molly. "There's no rush to get through them all." I wanted to proceed slowly, to carefully consider which items, if any, to carry in the shop and which to pass along to others, perhaps offering them to local teachers or the music department of the high school. Not all of the items were music-related, either. There were some pieces of men's clothing, a few books, some random household items. Those we set aside to pass along to Heidi.

On Friday we closed the shop early and walked to the MacTavish home. Rose, now back from visiting her relative, had come through with a violin for Molly to borrow, as I'd suspected she would.

"It's had a lot of use over the years, but I've inspected, tuned, and polished it," she told Molly. "It should serve you well."

"Gosh. Thank you so much." Molly picked up the instrument, made a few exploratory plucks on the strings, and signaled her satisfaction with a nod.

"Happy to help a musician in need."

"I'll take excellent care of it."

"I'm sure you will. Now, can I interest you ladies in a cup of tea? I was just about to give Emil his afternoon milk and cookies."

"Thank you, Rose," I said, "but we don't want to miss the wagon to camp."

"Of course." Rose bid us good-bye from her porch, little Emil tugging at her skirt. Molly and I made our way to the ramshackle shed on the edge of town where the lumber wagon-turned-shuttle bus sat ready to carry passengers up the mountain. The rickety old wagon awaited us, its weathered exterior a testament to years of hard use.

"It's a bit rough." I tugged the hem of my long skirt where it had snagged on a random nail. "But it's the quickest way up to Camp Harmony."

The wagoneer shouted "Giddyup," and the wagon lurched into motion. I stifled a grin at Molly's wide-eyed expression as we bounced along the rutted road. The scenery transformed from town buildings to lush forest, the air growing cooler as we climbed.

Before we even passed under the "Welcome to Camp Harmony" sign, we were greeted by the delightful snatches of music drifting through the air from the various cabins. We thanked the wagoneer, and I gave Molly a quick tour of the grounds. Young people roamed everywhere, walking and talking in twos and threes, playing a vigorous game of blind-man's-bluff, toting all manner of musical instruments to and from cabins. It felt strange and sad to see the beautiful flower beds and remember that Ernie was no longer around to care for them.

At the camp office in the main lodge, Carrie stood and circled her desk to greet us.

"Amanda! And this must be Molly." She pulled us both into a warm embrace. "I've heard so much about you. What do you think of our little camp?"

"What I've seen of it is lovely." Molly's eyes shone.

We settled onto a sofa. Carrie poured us some tea, and I told her about the crates of musical paraphernalia from Ernie's shed that had landed in my shop.

"I don't know if any of it would be of use to the camp," I said, "But you're welcome to come and take a look."

"Maybe I will, when the season is over. I'm needed here twenty-four hours a day, seven days a week. Why, I scarcely even get to see my husband. He helps as much as he can, but he still has the bank to run and must spend most days in town."

"Of course." My mind flickered with an unwelcome image of

Michael Tate and Heidi Fischer sharing a lunch in the hotel restaurant. Darn that Mildred Abernathy! I brushed the thought from my mind and broached the subject of Molly's musical talents. "Carrie, as we discussed earlier, I was wondering if there might be a place for another violinist in the camp orchestra this year."

Carrie's eyes lit up. "Well now, that's an interesting idea. The conductor is always on the lookout for fresh talent. What do you say, Molly? Care to audition?"

Molly's nervous excitement was palpable as we made our way to the rehearsal space. Dieter, looking relaxed and appropriately outdoorsy in an open-necked white shirt and casual trousers, greeted us with a smile that made my heart skip a beat. I hoped he was finding the fresh air and gentle pace of camp life refreshing after all the tough times he'd been through. He was indeed as distinguished-looking as I'd remembered from the banquet. It hadn't been the lantern-light playing tricks on my eyes.

Carrie explained to him the reason for our visit.

"So, young lady, you'd like to play in our orchestra," Dieter said to Molly in a more formal tone than he'd used with me.

She nodded.

"May I see your instrument, please?"

She set the violin case on a table and opened it. "This one isn't mine. It's on loan from Aunt Amanda's friend. Mine got broken on the train." Her voice hitched a little on that last sentence.

"I am very sorry to hear that." He looked at her for a long moment. "A tragedy."

"It's not as if my violin was particularly valuable, or anything like that," Molly hastened to say. "I just liked it, that's all. I'd grown accustomed to it."

Dieter's eyes grew misty. "Our instruments become a part of us, do they not? Losing it can feel like losing a limb ... or a loved one."

Dieter's words were kind and sympathetic, if a tad overdramatic. Ah, the romantic tendency of the artistic temperament.

Molly handed the violin to Dieter.

I watched, nerves on edge, as he turned the instrument over, his expression unreadable. What if he found it unacceptable?

He plucked a string, ran his fingers along the wood, and peered into the f-holes. After what felt like an eternity, he handed it back to Molly with a noncommittal "Hmm."

Molly shot me a worried glance before asking, "Is... is there something wrong with it?"

Dieter shrugged and resumed his formal manner. "It is an instrument. Whether it is good or not depends on the player. Why don't you play something for me? Let us hear what you can do."

Molly hesitated for a moment, her face rosy from more than just the summer heat. She tucked the violin under her chin, raised her bow, and launched into a Bach sonata.

As the music filled the room, Dieter's expression softened again. His foot tapped in time with the music, and a small smile played at the corners of his mouth.

When she finished, there was a moment of awed silence.

"Impressive." Dieter's eyes briefly met mine.

A warm sensation crept up my neck.

He turned his attention back to Molly. "You have talent, Miss Mulroney. I'd be delighted to have you join us for rehearsals and perform in our grand finale concert."

He winked at me, and I winked back, relieved that things had worked out. A weight I hadn't realized I was carrying lifted from my shoulders.

To my surprise, Molly's response seemed less animated than I expected. She gave a polite nod, but her expression was stoic. Perhaps she felt intimidated by the conductor's commanding presence.

As we discussed the rehearsal schedule and other details, Dieter kept sending glances my way. Each time our eyes met, a tiny winged creature fluttered in my chest. However, I also caught Molly watching these interactions with an odd expression I couldn't quite place.

Too soon, it was time to leave. Dieter walked us to the door. "I look forward to seeing you both at rehearsals." His gaze lingered on me a moment longer than necessary. "Surely you'll want to sit in and observe, Amanda. At least occasionally."

I hadn't planned on it, but found myself mentally adjusting my plans. If the maestro wanted me to observe rehearsals once in a while, then by golly, the least I could do was oblige.

He walked us to the wagon and gave us a hand up to our seats, Molly first, then me. He held onto my hand for a moment as his eyes sought mine. "I was so sorry to learn of the demise of Mr. Weiss," he murmured. "I can tell he was much appreciated by everyone here at the camp. And by you."

"Thank you." I swallowed. "Were you ever able to speak with him? You know, about the flowers?"

"Alas, we were only able to have one conversation before he—well." He paused, then added in a brighter tone, "Have dinner with me? Soon? We can discuss your memories of Mr. Weiss and ... and other topics."

My pulse accelerated. "I'd like that."

On the wagon ride back to town, I expected Molly to chatter with delight about her successful audition and opportunity to perform, but she seemed uncharacteristically quiet.

I nudged her shoulder with mine. "Is everything all right? You don't seem as excited as I thought you'd be."

Molly hesitated before responding. "I'm not sure, Aunt Amanda. Something about Mr. Volkov just... I don't know. He seems nice enough, but I got a strange feeling from him. He seems... cold. I can't explain it."

Cold was the last adjective I would have applied to Dieter. Her reaction mystified me. "Really? I think he's quite debonair. And he was clearly impressed by your playing. But maybe he's more ... authoritative with members of his orchestra. Most conductors are."

Molly shrugged, looking uncomfortable. "Maybe I'm just being silly. It's probably nothing."

We rode in silence for a while. My mind kept drifted between Molly's unexpected reaction and Dieter's warm brown eyes. I found myself anticipating our next visit to Camp Harmony, though now my eagerness was dampened a bit by Molly's unease.

I didn't believe her assessment of Dieter was correct.

Didn't *want* to believe it.

The sun dipped in the west as the wagon ambled along, and a cool breeze carried the scent of pine from the forest. Buttoning my cardigan against the chill, I turned to my niece.

"Anything else on your mind?"

"Now that I've met Mr. Volkov, I can't stop thinking about that anonymous letter the board received. The one asking the board to disinvite Stuart von Bauer from the music camp. I know it's probably old news by now, but it still bothers me deeply."

"I know, sweetie. And, sorry to say, it's not old news. To my knowledge, the sheriff still has no leads on who wrote it. It's a difficult situation." Though I'd told Molly about the poison-pen letter, I'd passed the actual letter along to James for the sheriff department's evidence file and felt glad to be rid of it.

She huffed. "It's not just difficult, it's wrong. How can people punish someone simply because of where they were born? The idea that no foreigner is to be trusted, and that all Germans are suddenly suspected enemies... it's absurd and unjust."

Ah, the idealism of youth. My gaze drifting to the streetlamps as we approached the town limits. "I understand your feelings, Molly. But I don't think it's something you need to worry about."

"But it is," she insisted. "Have you heard about what happened to Herr Schreiber back in Chicago?"

"Reinhard Schreiber, the orchestra conductor?" The name was familiar from *Metronome*. "No. What happened?"

"He was arrested on suspicion of espionage." Molly's voice dropped. "He was teaching at the conservatory and directing the Windy City Opera Company—always kind, always respectful to his musicians."

"Espionage? That's absurd! What evidence—"

"His crime was refusing to remove German music from the orchestra's program." Molly's lips thinned. "That, and being born in Germany. They raided his home, claimed he was sending secret messages through musical scores. Now he's in an internment camp at Fort Oglethorpe, facing deportation."

The wagon floor seemed to tilt beneath my feet. "They arrested a man for... for conducting Beethoven?"

"I'm afraid so."

"And now it's spreading here." My voice shook. "First that anonymous letter about Stuart von Bauer, now whispers about Dieter..." The magnitude of it hit me—how quickly suspicion could poison everything, even music.

Molly squeezed my arm. "We'll have to be careful, Aunt Amanda. Not everyone sees music the way we do—as something that brings people together."

I thought of Herr Schreiber in his cell, of Dieter trying to make a new life here, of all the musicians who'd crossed oceans carrying nothing but their instruments and hope. "Then we'll just have to help them see it differently, won't we?"

So much fighting, all of a sudden. Fighting prejudice in our little town. Fighting for answers about Ernie's death.

Was his death just a tragic accident? An attack triggered by his German surname? Or something else?

As the sun dipped below the horizon, casting a fiery glow across the sky, I couldn't shake the chill that had settled in my bones. What other shadows were gathering in our little mountain town?

Chapter Ten

Not long after Molly's tryout, Dieter telephoned the shop.

"I have learned that your American Independence Day will take place next Tuesday," he said. "The camp will be providing a brass band to play music at the lakefront. I understand there will be a picnic, and fireworks. You will come?"

It wasn't exactly an invitation. More of a statement. But one to which I readily agreed.

"Yes, we'll be there. Molly and I."

"Oh. You have already made plans to go." He sounded disappointed.

"Well, yes, but we'll look for you. Maybe we can all sit together to watch the fireworks."

***

The early evening sun sparkled on Lake Collier like scattered diamonds as the good citizens of Timber Coulee gathered for the annual Fourth of July celebration. The scent of fried chicken and fresh-baked pies mingled with the sharp tang of gunpowder from the morning's cannon salute, and everywhere I looked, red, white, and blue bunting fluttered in the mountain breeze.

"This is delightful." Dieter stretched out his long legs on our checkered blanket. "All these people seated on the grass in their finest clothing. It reminds me of that Impressionist painting at the Art Institute. *A Sunday Afternoon on La Grande Jatte.*"

"Oh, I love that painting, and I agree with you." I glanced at him. "But when did you see it? You said you'd never been to Chicago."

His face reddened, almost imperceptibly. "I haven't. I saw a reproduction in a book of color plates, and it made an impression."

"I guess that's why they call it 'Impressionist,'" Molly drawled from her corner of the blanket, where she'd been unusually quiet. I laughed, but Dieter didn't. Instead he stared out over the lake, although his dark eyes were not focused on the aquamarine waves.

"In Russia, we had nothing like this... such innocent revelry." His accent caressed the words, making even *revelry* sound like music.

I smoothed my white lawn dress, conscious of how close he was sitting. "Well, Timber Coulee may be small, but we do know how to celebrate properly."

"Indeed you do." He smiled, reaching for another deviled egg. "These are extraordinary, Amanda. You must share your secret."

"Oh, those are mine, actually," Molly piped up. "Family recipe. Lots of mustard."

"Ah!" Dieter's dark eyes sparkled. "Then I must congratulate you, Miss Mulroney. You have quite a talent."

Molly's "thank you" was perfectly polite, but I caught the slight tightening around her mouth. She'd been oddly reserved all afternoon, nothing like her usual effervescent self.

The brass band struck up a spirited rendition of "The Stars and Stripes Forever," the music floating across the lake like sunshine given voice. I watched Dieter's fingers move slightly, conducting along with the melody.

"They play quite well for a small-town band," he observed. "Though the piccolo is a bit sharp."

"That's Izzy Parker." Molly sounded a touch defensive. "She takes lessons at the store. I think she plays beautifully."

When the band took their break, she jumped to her feet. "I think I'll go say hello to Izzy," she announced. "She looks warm—perhaps she'd like some lemonade."

I watched her pick her way through the crowd, her yellow muslin dress bright against the gathering dusk. "That's thoughtful of her," I said.

"Mmm." Dieter's noncommittal response was barely audible. He was gazing out across the lake, his expression distant. "The setting sun, how it sparkles... it reminds me of summer evenings floating in a rowboat on the Neva, the lights of my father's house shining on the water."

Poor Dieter. "You must miss your homeland terribly."

He turned to me, and something in his eyes made my heart flutter. "Less and less each day," he murmured. "Have I told you how lovely you look in white?"

Heat stole across my cheeks. We sat in contented silence as dusk fell. The first firework burst overhead with a whistle and a crack, painting the sky in brilliant red. I jumped, and Dieter's hand found mine in the darkness, his fingers warm and strong.

"Beautiful," he whispered, but when I glanced at him, he wasn't looking at the sky. I was glad for the darkness that obscured my blush.

Further down the shore, I could just make out Molly's yellow dress in the flickering light. She was sitting next to Izzy Parker on a fallen log, their heads bent skyward as they watched the display. Molly had made a friend. Something about their easy companionship warmed my heart.

And the other thing warming my heart was the way Dieter's hand enveloped mine, genteel and proper. Yet there was something in the careful way his fingers curled around my own that made my breath catch in my throat.

The fireworks painted the lake in flashes of gold and silver, each burst echoing off the mountains like distant thunder. In that moment, with the pressure of Dieter's hand in mine and the sky ablaze with color, I could almost forget the troubles that had been plaguing our little town.

Almost.

But even as I leaned slightly closer to Dieter's shoulder, I couldn't quite shake the memory of Molly's reserved expression, or the way her eyes had narrowed when Dieter mentioned Russia. My niece had always been uncommonly perceptive. Perhaps I should ask her again what was bothering her about our charming visitor.

Later, I told myself, as another burst of color illuminated Dieter's handsome profile. Some questions could wait until tomorrow.

***

The next morning, I pondered the tall stack of unsold New York Philharmonic gramophone records. Poor Stuart von Bauer. If he'd been able to keep his commitment, these records would have sold better. On the other hand, if he hadn't fallen ill, I wouldn't have met Dieter. Feeling both grateful for von Bauer's absence and guilty for being grateful, I shot up a quick prayer for the conductor's complete recovery.

I'd just posted a "half price" sign above the pile, humming snippets of last night's patriotic tunes, when Molly rushed in, her hat askew and her cheeks flushed.

"So sorry I'm late." She fumbled with her handbag, nearly dropping it. "I must have slept through my alarm."

"Well, well." I was unable to resist teasing. "Someone must have had quite an enjoyable evening. When last I noticed, you and that young trumpeter seemed rather absorbed in conversation beneath the fireworks."

Molly yanked her hat pin out with more force than necessary. "I don't see how that's any of your business," she snapped, then immediately looked contrite. "I'm sorry, I didn't mean—"

"Goodness," I said lightly, though her tone stung. "Someone woke up on the wrong side of the bed this morning."

"At least I wasn't making calf eyes at a complete stranger all evening," she muttered, attacking the sheet music with unnecessary vigor.

I set down my pencil with a sharp click. "I beg your pardon?"

"Oh, come now, Aunt Amanda." Molly turned to face me, her eyes bright with an emotion I couldn't quite read. "You can't tell me you actually believe all those romantic stories about Russian nobility and concert halls in Moscow."

"Saint Petersburg. And what exactly is wrong with Mr. Volkov's stories?" I could feel heat rising in my cheeks. "He's been nothing but polite and—"

"That's exactly it!" Molly burst out. "He's too polite. Too perfect. And the way he looked at you yesterday, like... like..." She broke off, shaking her head.

"Like what?" I demanded, my voice sharper than I'd intended.

"Really, Molly, I think you're being rather unfair. Just because some-one is refined and well-traveled doesn't mean—"

"Never mind," Molly cut in, turning back to the sheet music. "For-get I said anything. You clearly don't want to hear it."

I opened my mouth to retort, then caught myself. The wall clock ticked loudly in the sudden silence, its steady rhythm reminding me of all the times Ernie had counseled patience in moments of anger. "Perhaps," I said carefully, "I should take a brief walk. Clear my head a bit."

Molly's shoulders remained stiff, but I saw her hands falter slightly in their sorting. "The shop—"

"—will be fine in your capable hands for half an hour." I retrieved my copy of *Metronome* magazine from the drawer under the counter. "And Molly?" I paused, hand on the latch. "When I return, perhaps we could both try this conversation again? With less... heat?"

A ghost of a smile touched her lips. "Yes, ma'am."

The morning breeze was already warm as I stepped onto Main Street, but I welcomed its touch on my flushed cheeks. As I made my way toward the park, I couldn't help but wonder if there might be a grain of truth in Molly's concerns. She'd always been unusually perceptive, even as a child...

But no. Surely she was just being overprotective. Wasn't she?

A robin hopped along the path ahead of me, pecking at invisible treasures, and I found myself envying its simple concerns. When had life become so complicated? And why did my niece's words about Dieter leave me feeling so unsettled?

The park bench beneath a leafy tree beckoned, promising shade and solitude. Perhaps after I'd sat and read for a while, I'd be better equipped to navigate both Molly's mood and my own confused feel-ings about our handsome visitor.

I settled onto the bench, pulled the creased copy of *Metronome* from my bag, and tried to lose myself in the article about Camp Harmony's Silver Jubilee season. The article was well-written and complimentary to the camp, but instead of solace, I found myself worrying even more.

What devastating effect would it have on the camp if word spread of the rash of vandalism being committed around town? Parents would stop sending their children, fearing for their safety. Audiences would stay home. Panic might ensue. Timber Coulee would earn a bad reputation. And if that happened, who would come to my shop?

The warm breeze ruffled the magazine's pages. The scent of blooming roses wafted through the air, mingling with the earthy aroma of freshly mown grass. The article on Camp Harmony failed to hold my attention, but a second article titled "The Delicate Harmony of Genius and Madness" caught my eye.

The article delved into the often fragile mental state of musical prodigies, using several historical examples to illustrate its point. But one case study in particular gripped my attention.

> Perhaps no tale better exemplifies this phenomenon than the tragic story of Lucas Baker. In 1893, Baker was a seventeen-year-old violin virtuoso whose mastery of the instrument belied his tender years. Critics hailed him as the next Paganini, and his future seemed as bright as the polished wood of his beloved Stradivarius.

> But fate had other plans. Baker's father, a notorious

gambler, sold the boy's prized violin to cover his debts. The loss shattered young Lucas. In a fit of desperation, he attacked the acclaimed virtuoso Imogene Lansdorf, who had unwittingly purchased the instrument. Baker's attempt to reclaim his violin failed, and he was promptly institutionalized.

Adding to the mystery, an unidentified accomplice escaped with the violin during the commotion. To this day, the valuable instrument's whereabouts remain unknown.

I lowered the magazine, my mind whirling. How could someone become so attached to an instrument that losing it would drive them to such extremes? How would I feel if my own cello was wrenched out of my arms? I'd hate that. But even then, I couldn't fathom resorting to violence.

My heart ached for the young Lucas Baker. To have such immense talent, such promise, only to have it all stripped away in an instant—it was truly tragic. What became of him after his institutionalization? Did he ever play again? Did the loss of his beloved violin haunt him forever?

Goosebumps rose on my arms despite the warm day. There was something unsettling about the story, something that nagged at the edges of my mind. But I couldn't put my finger on what it was.

***

A few days later, Dieter again telephoned the shop and invited me to dinner on Saturday. We arranged to meet at Mountain Melodies before our date. So far, most of our encounters had taken place on either his turf or neutral territory. It was about time he saw me in my natural habitat. It mattered a great deal to me that he'd approve of my little shop. I didn't know *why* it mattered, but it did. As an extension of myself, I supposed. Love me, love my shop.

Except *love* was a little premature. Perhaps a lot premature. Thankfully, I hadn't uttered the word aloud in his presence. I'd need to guard my tongue. Not to mention my heart.

Since time didn't permit me to go home first, I'd changed into my white dress at lunchtime, then covered it with an apron for the afternoon's work. Now, well past closing time, I adjusted the neckline and fidgeted with my hair. The hour grew later. I worried he wasn't coming.

Moxie draped the length of his furry orange self across the counter, his tail swishing lazily as he kept a watchful eye on the door. He seemed to sense my nervousness, offering an occasional soft meow of reassurance.

At last Dieter appeared, backlit by the golden twilight as he strode past the display window. Dressed in a sky-blue linen suit and straw boater hat, his tall figure cut a dashing silhouette.

My anxiety melted away as I unlocked the door and pulled it open.

"Amanda," he exclaimed. "How enchanting you look." The appreciative look in his eyes made me overlook his lack of apology for being late. Besides, it probably wasn't his fault. The camp wagon was a slow-going beast at the best of times.

"Thank you." I swept my arm in an exaggerated arc. "Welcome, maestro, to Mountain Melodies."

"What a lovely little place you have here." As Dieter strode into the shop, Moxie's easygoing demeanor made an abrupt change. His fur bristled, and he let out a low, menacing growl. I was taken aback. My cat was usually so friendly with customers.

"Oh, Moxie, hush now," I scolded gently, embarrassed by his behavior.

Dieter's posture stiffened. "In my country, cats are valued for chasing mice."

"They're valued for that here, too, when they aren't being lazy. Or rude." I gave the cat a warning look.

"You called it Moxie. That is the name of a fountain drink, is it not?"

"Yes, but it's also a slang word that means to show courage or nerve." A *lot* of nerve, at the moment.

Moxie hissed, his tail puffing up to twice its size.

"I'm so sorry." Mortification choked my words. "He's not usually like this. Moxie, shoo! Go on, get down from there."

Moxie reluctantly jumped off the counter and slinked behind the piano, his eyes never leaving Dieter.

"No need to apologize," Dieter soothed, though he kept a wary eye on Moxie's hiding spot. "Animals can be... unpredictable."

In an effort to move past the awkward moment, I tried to laugh, but it came out like more of a strangled gasp. Our evening wasn't getting off to the smoothest start.

Dieter's keen eyes swept the room as if cataloging every instrument. He asked a few businesslike questions about the inventory and the clientele. Then he remarked, "It surprises me that you have no violins on display." His tone was vaguely accusatory, as though my lack of violins was a personal shortcoming. Of course, it made sense he'd focus in on his favorite instrument.

"Not at the moment," I said. "Sorry."

"Ah, well, you see, we have a bit of a predicament at the camp. Young Timothy Hawkins has shown quite the aptitude for the violin, but alas, he has no instrument of his own."

"Oh, how wonderful that he's found his calling." Timothy was a local boy who seemed prone to shyness. "But I'm afraid I don't have any violins in stock at the moment. I'm waiting on a shipment that was supposed to arrive last week. I can't imagine what's caused the delay, but I haven't had time to telephone the vendor and ask."

Was it my imagination, or did a flicker of disappointment cross Dieter's noble features? But it was gone in an instant, replaced by his usual disarming smile.

"No matter, no matter." He waved a dismissive hand. "Perhaps we can make do with one of the camp's instruments for now." Casually, he picked up a trumpet and examined it.

Instinct made me hope he wouldn't put fingerprints all over it, then I chided myself for the thought.

"But tell me, Amanda," he continued, "Have you acquired any interesting pieces lately? Any, shall we say, antique instruments?"

I shook my head. "I'm afraid not. Just the usual assortment of guitars, mandolins, and the odd banjo or two. And we did receive a clarinet and a piccolo from Ernie Weiss's estate, along with his guitar. But I wouldn't call them antiques. Just kind of old."

"Is that all?" His gaze flicked around the room, as if expecting to spot something I'd overlooked. "A pity."

His critical attitude began to dampen my enthusiasm for our date. "If it's antiques you're interested in, I suggest you visit Elite Repeat, three doors down. They carry lots of old things. In fact, they're handling most of Ernie's Weiss's estate, including his extensive tool collection. You might find something there for your garden. And the proceeds will go toward a scholarship program for Camp Harmony."

"A worthy cause." He replaced the trumpet on its stand.

From beneath the piano, Moxie let out another low growl.

I shot him a stern look, silently willing him to behave.

Dieter continued, seeming unperturbed by Moxie's hostile behavior. "Well, I suppose we should be getting along to dinner. I have developed quite the appetite, have you?"

"All set," I replied, trying to shake off a brief sense of letdown that coursed through me. I'd so wanted to impress him, but I didn't seem to have anything he wanted. And Moxie's behavior had been mortifying. What had happened to my sweet feline friend?

As I gathered my wrap and evening bag, said animal darted out from his hiding place and positioned himself between Dieter and me. His tail was still puffed, and he fixed the maestro with a baleful stare.

"Moxie, enough!" I shooed him away. "I'm so sorry about his behavior, Dieter. I can't imagine what's gotten into him."

"It's quite all right," Dieter assured me, though he kept a wary eye on Moxie as we made our way to the door.

I locked up behind us, and as we headed toward the hotel, I caught a whiff of his cologne—a spicy, exotic scent that made me think of faraway places. Maybe that was it—the unfamiliar scent had, for some reason, enraged Moxie and turned him into a ferocious jungle beast. In any case, I determined to set my injured feelings aside and have a good time. After all, I rationalized, my little shop couldn't be everything to everybody. It was there to serve the local community and the camp, not the occasional big shot accustomed to a more splendid array of merchandise. And Dieter had plenty of attractive qualities to outweigh the occasional minor annoyance.

Still, as we walked arm in arm down the street, I couldn't quite shake the memory of Moxie's unusual behavior. In all the years since the cat had adopted me as his human, I'd never seen him react so strongly to a stranger. But surely it didn't mean anything... did it?

My sense of unease soon dissipated in the romantic setting of Timber Coulee's finest—and only—restaurant, although the soft glow of candles on each table was marred somewhat by the Majestic Theater's new electric lights blazing across the street, advertising the latest Charlie Chaplin picture show. Yet another example of so-called "progress."

Over the rim of his wine glass, the garnet-colored liquid catching the flickering candlelight, Dieter's dark eyes met mine.

"Amanda." His voice caressed my name in a way that made me blush, the low timbre of his voice sending a pleasant shiver down my spine. "I must confess, I find myself quite enchanted by you."

I gave an unladylike snort, shielding my awkward pleasure behind a napkin that felt crisp and cool against my warming cheeks. "Surely a worldly man like yourself has known far more fascinating women than a small-town music shop owner."

His expression sobered, and he reached across the table to take my hand. The touch of his callused fingertips sent a tingle up my arm. "You would be surprised." His thumb traced small circles on my palm. "I have known many people in my life, but few with your warmth and genuine spirit."

Something in his tone made me curious. The clink of cutlery and the soft murmur of conversation from nearby tables faded into the background as I leaned in, drawn by the intensity of his gaze. Time to take the focus off myself and onto him. "Tell me about your life before you came here." The words came out in a near whisper. "Tell me more about Russia."

Dieter's eyes grew distant, as if looking into a past I couldn't see. He took a sip of his wine. His throat moved as he swallowed. "Ah, yes. Russia. It seems like another lifetime now." He swirled the wine in his glass, the motion hypnotic in the candlelight. "I grew up in St.

Petersburg, you see. My father was a prosperous businessman, and we lived in a grand house overlooking the Neva River. Those were bright, happy days, filled with music and laughter."

His words captivated me, drew me into his story. We might as well have been alone in the restaurant. "It sounds wonderful. What happened?"

His expression darkened, a shadow passing over his aquiline features like a cloud obscuring the sun. "Our country was already destabilized from years of tensions among different groups of citizens. Only a few years ago, we survived a failed uprising against the wealthier class, men like my father. When Russia joined the Allies in the war against Germany, these tensions worsened by the day. We barely escaped with our lives." He paused, and just as I was wondering if "we" indicated he had a wife and a family tucked away somewhere, a flicker of pain crossed his face, with an almost imperceptible tightening of his jaw. "I made my way to America alone, determined to start anew."

There was my answer. *Alone. Whew.* "Oh, Dieter," I breathed, squeezing his hand, feeling the strength in his fingers as they curled around mine. "I'm so sorry. That must have been terribly difficult."

He gave a bittersweet grimace which remained shadowed with memories. "It was, but I persevered. Music was my solace. I practiced day and night, until my fingers bled and my shoulders ached, and eventually, I was hired as a violinist with the Cincinnati Symphony."

"Cincinnati?" I repeated, the word feeling odd on my tongue. "But I thought—"

"I have been very fortunate," Dieter continued, not seeming to notice my interruption. His voice took on a dreamy quality, and I could almost hear the phantom strains of an orchestra. "Things could have turned out much worse for me. But I yearned for something more... intimate. When I heard about this charming music camp in

Idaho, I hoped it would be the perfect opportunity." His eyes locked with mine as if searching my soul. "And now, I know it was."

A flutter of panic beat against my ribcage. It had been a long time since anyone had looked at me that way.

"I'll bet you say that to all the cellists," I joked as I withdrew my hand from his.

He looked like an injured puppy "No, I do not. Why would you say that?"

"Sorry. Bad joke." I took a sip of water.

His expression turned stony. "You are sorry I came."

"Oh, Dieter. Of course not." My goodness, he was sensitive. That artistic temperament again. "I'll admit, I was disappointed when Stuart von Bauer had to cancel. But I'm not sorry now. I'm glad you came."

His smile returned. "So am I."

Eager to exit the swampy territory of deep feelings, I said, "Speaking of the camp, have you decided on the program for the grand finale concert? I'm sure everyone in town is eager to know what to expect."

Dieter's eyes lit up. "Ah, yes! I am thrilled to announce that we'll be performing selections from various Tchaikovsky compositions, including *Swan Lake*. It is a personal favorite of mine. And it reminds me of our day together at Lake Collier."

"Oh, how wonderful!" To my relief, we'd returned to the safe conversational ground of our shared love of music. "*Swan Lake* is such a beautiful piece. The campers must be excited to tackle such a challenging work."

"Indeed, they are. The music is technically demanding, but also deeply emotional. It is a perfect showcase for their talents. In fact, I've decided to give a violin solo to your niece."

"Have you? She didn't tell me."

"It is possible she meant for it to be a surprise. I do hope I haven't spoiled anything."

"You haven't. I won't say a word," I assured him. "I've always been fascinated by the story behind *Swan Lake*. The tragedy, the romance, the transformation..."

"Tchaikovsky's life was equally fascinating," Dieter said. "Have you ever read his biography?"

I shook my head. "No, I'm afraid I haven't had the pleasure."

"Oh, you must! I brought a copy with me to Idaho. Would you like to borrow it? I think you'd find it illuminating, especially in relation to *Swan Lake*."

"That's very kind of you. I'd love to read it."

"Excellent." That intriguing dimple flashed in his cheek. "I'll bring it to your shop tomorrow. Perhaps we can discuss it over coffee once you've finished."

So he wanted to see me again. The thought brought a glow to my insides. Slow and steady. Get to know one another over time. That was the ticket. No more of this breathless-hypnotic-gaze business.

But as he spoke, I once again found myself drawn into the depths of his eyes, so full of mystery and unspoken stories. The rest of the evening passed in a blur of shared laughter and lingering glances, the taste of a rich chocolate dessert and the warmth of aged brandy lingering on my tongue. When he walked me to my door at the end of the night, the cool mountain air nipped at our cheeks, carrying the scent of pine and distant wildflowers. I felt weightless, floating, my skin tingling where his hand rested lightly on the small of my back.

"Well, good night, Amanda. I had a lovely evening."

"So did I. Good night."

It wasn't until later, as I was preparing for bed, the quiet of the house broken only by the ticking of the old grandfather clock in the hall, that a nagging thought resurfaced. Hadn't Carrie mentioned Dieter was with the Cleveland Symphony? Yet tonight he'd said Cincinnati. *Oh, what difference does it make?* I shook my head, smirking at my own confusion as I ran a brush through my hair. Perhaps I'd misheard, or perhaps Carrie had been mistaken. Either way, Ohio was Ohio. And a long, long distance from Idaho.

Moxie wound himself around my ankles, his soft purr a soothing counterpoint to my whirling thoughts. I bent to scratch behind his ears, much as he didn't deserve it after his behavior earlier in the evening. "Well, Mr. Moxie," I mumbled, "Molly must have let you in tonight. I don't know that *I* would have. I don't need to ask what you thought of Mr. Volkov. You weren't very nice to him, you know." His only response was to butt his head against my hand, demanding more attention.

As I slipped into bed, the unrepentant animal hopped up to claim his usual spot at my feet.

"Oh, so now you decide to be all cute and cuddly." His blinking stare held no apology. Even so, his warm weight was a comforting presence against my legs.

The brandy must have muddled my memory concerning the two Ohio cities. After all, they both started with C. Or perhaps Carrie had been mistaken. She had been more than a little flustered on the night of the banquet.

As Moxie's gentle purring lulled me to dreamland, my thoughts filled with images of a grand Russian estate and the haunting strains of a violin. But somewhere in the back of my mind, a small voice whispered that something wasn't quite right. I pushed the thought away, choosing instead to bask in the warm glow of a budding romance, the softness of my pillow cradling my cheek as I slipped into slumber.

Chapter Eleven

A soft summer rain pattered against the windows of my cottage, casting a cozy mood over the front room. Heaven knew we needed the rain. So far, July had been quite dry.

Molly was at rehearsal. Alone except for Moxie, I'd decided to fill the quiet evening by going through the last of Ernie's old crates, which earlier I'd carried home from the shop.

Sitting cross-legged on the floor, I used a kitchen utensil to pry open the crate, a smallish one decorated with a smiling tomato. Inside was a rolled-up blanket. I lifted it out of the crate with care. What could it be? Nothing else had been wrapped this way. For one wild moment I feared it might be something dreadful, like the skeleton of a beloved pet, and nearly thrust it back into the crate. But curiosity made me pull back the cloth.

"Would you look at that?" I whispered to Moxie. It was a beautiful instrument—a violin. Despite a missing bridge and strings, there was potential beneath its years of neglect.

"Gracious." My fingers slid against smooth wood. "Can you imagine?" I looked at Moxie and shook my head. "Who would store something like this in a dirty old fruit crate? It's not in great shape... but I'd say it's quite a find, wouldn't you?"

The cat twitched his whiskers as if comprehending my running commentary.

"Tell you what. Since we're already planning to take Molly's violin in for repairs, we'll take this one in as well. See if Floyd Hendricks can do anything with it. If he can, then Molly will have multiple violins to choose from. If she doesn't want it, I can sell it in the shop."

Should I mention it to Dieter? After all, he'd been interested in procuring a violin for Timothy. No, the instrument was in too poor a condition to be useful, and besides, I was still smarting a little from the maestro's oblique criticism of my shop and felt in no rush to fulfill his wishes. He'd likely scoff at an old violin that had been stuffed into a fruit crate for who knows how many years.

Moxie sat up and stretched. Suddenly, he leaped to the floor and started batting something near my feet with his paw.

A scrap of letter paper had fluttered to the floor. I retrieved it, my fingers brushing against the rough, timeworn edge. "What have we here?" I murmured more to myself than to the cat.

The handwriting was spidery and urgent, the ink faded but still legible.

Do not bring it here. This is a dangerous place and it will not be safe. Guard it with your life, and when I am free, I will come to you and we will settle our business.

That was all it said. Curiosity seized me. Who had written it? The handwriting was distinctive—an elegant and flowing Spencerian style popular in the nineteenth century, with ornate capital letters, indicating the writer had received a formal education, if an old-fashioned one. And what was the "it" referred to? Surely there was more to the message than this. I pawed through the crate to see if I might have overlooked the first page of a letter or something, but found nothing. There was no signature, no envelope, nothing to indicate who had written these cryptic words or to whom they were addressed. But as

I turned the scrap of stationery over in my hands, my heart began to race. There, imprinted on the reverse side, were six words that sent a chill rippling through my body, like a stone dropped into a river.

Northern Illinois Asylum for the Insane.

I knew of this place—a state institution located some forty miles outside of Chicago. What was Ernie's connection to the hospital? Had his wife spent time there? Had *Ernie* spent time there?

"Oh, Ernie." I sank back. "What on earth were you mixed up in?"

Moxie, sensing my distress, leaped onto my lap with a soft meow. I absently stroked his fur as my mind whirled with possibilities. This note ... how was it connected to something in the crates? Or to Ernie?

The rain had stopped and the clouds parted. As moonlight glowed through the window, I couldn't shake the feeling that this scrap of paper was about to change everything. The quiet strains of a distant violin seemed to echo in my mind, a haunting melody of secrets long buried and truths yet to be revealed.

The next day, after a restless night, I was still mulling over the question of Ernie's connection to the asylum when a customer entered the shop, startling me from my thoughts. I shoved the note into my skirt pocket to ponder later.

"Good afternoon. Welcome to Mountain Melodies." The young man's shirt pocket had the Camp Harmony insignia stitched on it. I came around the counter wearing my warmest smile. Campers were my favorite customers.

"Are you Miss Parrish?" The boy peered at me with suspicion, as though I might try to misrepresent my identity.

"Yes, I am. Can I help you find something?"

"Well, I ain't —*am not*—here to buy nothing."

The boy's tone was sullen. "Maestro found out I was headed to town and told me to give this to you."

He handed me a thick clothbound book—the biography of Tchaikovsky Dieter had recommended to me. A twinge of disappointment pricked my heart that he hadn't delivered it himself, but I supposed he was very busy at the camp. At least he'd remembered his promise to lend it to me—which meant he'd been thinking of me. I thanked the boy and slipped the book into my bag to take home.

The mysterious scrap of a note and my sadness over Ernie, not to mention mean-spirited, foreigner-hating vandals lurking somewhere in Timber Coulee, made it hard to concentrate on my bookkeeping, but I did my best. Around mid-morning Molly breezed into the shop, her cheeks flushed and hair windswept.

"Molly!" I took in her disheveled appearance. "Where on earth have you been? And what in heaven's name are you wearing?"

She grinned, striking a pose in her divided skirt, a potential scandal in Timber Coulee if there ever was one. No doubt tongues had started wagging already. "Isn't it marvelous? It's a divided skirt! Perfect for riding my new bicycle!"

I blinked, sure I had misheard. "Your new what?"

"My bicycle!" Molly's eyes sparkled with excitement. "I just rode it up to the camp and back. You wouldn't believe the view from up there!"

The ledger forgotten, I hurried around the counter, the floorboards creaking under my feet. "Molly Mulroney, are you telling me you rode a bicycle all the way up the mountain? Alone?"

"Oh, don't be such a wet blanket." Molly laughed, helping herself to a glass of water from the canister kept at the back of the store. She took a long sip. "It was perfectly safe. And exhilarating!"

A headache crept into my temples. "Molly, that's miles of steep, winding road. It's far too strenuous and dangerous for a young lady to attempt alone."

Molly's smile faded, replaced by a look of stubborn determination I knew all too well. "Aunt Amanda, I'm not some delicate flower that needs protecting. I'm perfectly capable of handling a bicycle ride."

"I'm not saying you're not capable." I fought to keep my voice level. "I'm simply concerned for your safety. What if you had an accident? Or if some ne'er-do-well—"

"Oh, for heaven's sake!" Molly rolled her eyes. "You sound positively Victorian. It's nineteen-sixteen. Women are doing all sorts of things these days. Working in factories, driving automobiles, even flying airplanes!"

Her words stung, but I tried not to let it show. After all, did I not pride myself on being a modern, independent woman? Didn't I run my own business? Hadn't I embraced the typewriter and the telephone? But still, there was modern and then there was... well, Molly.

"I'm well aware of the date, thank you very much," I replied, perhaps with a bit more tartness than I intended. "And I'll remind you I'm quite modern myself. But there's a difference between being modern and being reckless."

Molly's expression softened a bit. "I know you keep up to date, Aunt Amanda. And I'm sorry if I implied otherwise. But you have to admit, sometimes you can be a bit... old-fashioned. For a moment there, you almost sounded like Mother."

I closed my mouth. Much as I loved my sister, Kathleen, I didn't relish sounding like her. The ticking of the clock on the wall seemed to grow louder in the sudden silence.

"Perhaps you're right," I admitted at last. "But that doesn't change the fact that I worry about you."

Molly gave me a quick hug. "I know you do, and I appreciate it. But you have to let me spread my wings a little."

I held her at arm's length. "All right, here's what we'll do. You're free to ride your bicycle as much as you like."

Her face lit up, but I held up a hand to stop her before she could speak.

"But you are not to ride down that mountain alone after dark. Is that clear?"

Molly opened her mouth as if to argue, then closed it again. After a moment, she nodded. "That's fair, I suppose. No night rides down the mountain alone. I promise."

"Good." Relief untied the knot my shoulders. "Now, why don't you tell me all about this marvelous view from the camp? And perhaps explain to me how exactly one rides a bicycle in that... divided skirt. And where can I buy one?"

Molly laughed, the tension evaporating like morning dew. As she launched into an animated description of her adventure, I couldn't help but shake my head in fond exasperation. Heaven help me if solving Ernie's mystery was going to be anywhere near as challenging as keeping up with my thoroughly modern niece.

Thinking of Ernie reminded me of the note in my pocket. Molly stopped short and peered at me. "What's wrong? You look as if you've seen a phantom."

I managed a weak smile. "Not a phantom. But perhaps ... a message from the past."

As I recounted my discovery—well, Moxie's discovery, to be fair—and showed Molly the note, she became transfixed. "But what does it mean? Who do you think wrote it? And why was it hidden in Ernie's crate?"

"That's the million-dollar question, Molly-girl. I wish I knew. But I do know that the Northern Illinois Asylum for the Insane is located near Chicago, only more recently it's called the Elgin State Hospital.

That would indicate that the note I found is at least ten years old, if not more, because it bore the old name of the hospital."

"But Ernie wasn't in Illinois then, was he? He was here in Idaho."

"I don't know. That was before I knew him, and he never spoke much about his past." I set the note on the counter. "I have a feeling we're just beginning to unravel the true story of Ernie Weiss."

Later that night, I couldn't sleep for thinking of Ernie. Remembering my promise to arrange one of his songs for the Mountain Meadowlarks, I tiptoed downstairs, sat at the kitchen table, and smoothed open the well-worn leather cover of his songwriting notebook, its corners softened from much use. The pages were wavy from coffee and water stains. Loose pages of different sizes were tucked at random between the bound sheets, some containing hastily scrawled lyrics while others held more carefully notated musical scores. Some of the songs looked familiar to me, others not.

Molly wandered into the kitchen, dressed her robe. "Can't sleep?"

"Nope."

"Me neither." She pulled out a chair and sat. "I keep playing *Swan Lake* over and over in my head, trying to get the fingering right. Whatcha got there?"

"Ernie's notebook. It's where he worked out all his song lyrics and guitar chords."

"Keen!" She leaned in to get a closer look. "Good luck deciphering that chicken scratch."

She had a point. Ernie's handwriting started neat on each page but grew messier as his ideas flowed.

"Shall I make us some tea?" she asked.

"No, thanks. That would *really* keep me awake."

"Good point. Well, I'll leave you to it." She stood. "I'll try reading that detective novel I found at Elite Repeat. If nothing else, it'll keep my mind off *Swan Lake*."

Her footsteps padded up the stairs as I returned to the notebook and sank into its dog-eared pages, searching for something appropriate for the Meadowlarks. A song that would do justice to Ernie's memory—and also sound great in four-part harmony, with Beatrice Fairmont's paint-peeling soprano in the lead.

Time passed. A headache formed in my temples. I'd been at work for well over an hour, and something wasn't normal about these songs.

Take "Signals in the Night." He'd written at least four versions, which wasn't unusual for a songwriter. But the changes between versions made no sense musically. Why change "red and green against the sky" to "yellow and green against the sky" when the first version had better rhythm? And why note specifically that the westbound train in verse one became eastbound in verse three?

I flipped back to his children's counting song. Sweet and simple, the kind Sunday school children would enjoy. But then, twenty pages later, another version appeared with darker lyrics about agents and watchers and burned letters.

My skin prickled. In the margins were numbers: 3-1-4-2-7. They seemed so random. I assumed they had meaning only to him.

Blame it on the lateness of the hour and the lack of sleep. Or on Molly's mention of a detective novel.

I grabbed a pencil and paper. If those numbers matched up to words in each line... I ran my finger along the third word of line one: "blackbird." First word of line two: "Two." Fourth word of line three: "wave." Second word of line four: "the." Seventh word of line five...

The stairs creaked. I slammed the notebook shut as Molly drifted in, hair askew. She squinted at me.

"I saw the light still on. Why aren't you in bed yet?" She yawned.

"Soon." I slid my paper under the notebook. "Still working on that music for the Meadowlarks. I'm hitting on all sixes and don't want to stop."

"Well, as long as you're all right ..." She headed back upstairs.

I waited until her footsteps faded, then opened the notebook again. My hands shook. Because unless I was imagining things, Ernie Weiss hadn't just been writing songs.

He'd been leaving messages. Messages concerning railroads, and other things that seemed to make no sense.

But who for? And had someone killed him for them?

Chapter Twelve

In the bright light of morning, the "messages" I'd discovered in Ernie's notebook seemed as silly and nonsensical as... well, as a detective novel, and a badly written one at that. Maybe I'd dozed off at the table and dreamed them. In any case, I was glad I hadn't said anything about them to Molly, as she'd no doubt think me quite the doddering fool.

As soon as we were dressed, she and I set out for Elite Repeat in search of a few things to make her room more homey. She'd fallen in love with Heidi's shop on our first visit. As we strolled down Main Street, the cool mountain air nipped at our cheeks, promising another beautiful summer day in Timber Coulee.

"I can't wait to see what treasures we'll find." Molly's enthusiasm was infectious, and I found myself smiling despite the early hour.

We reached the storefront, its windows still dark. *Strange.* Heidi was usually an early riser.

"Maybe she overslept?" Molly said.

I tried the door, surprised to find it unlocked. A wave of concern washed over me as we stepped inside. "Heidi? Are you here?" I half expected Michael Tate to step out, as he had before, then scolded myself for entertaining such a notion. Whatever reason he'd had for visiting Heidi that day was no concern of mine.

The shop was eerily quiet. As my eyes adjusted to the dimness, I gasped in horror. The place was in utter disarray—shelves toppled, clothes strewn about, and trinkets scattered across the floor. The shop's normal state was a little cluttered, part of the charm of a secondhand shop, but this was madness.

Similar to the state of Ernie Weiss's house.

"Aunt Amanda." Molly pointed, her voice a shaky whisper. "Look!"

My heart thudded in my chest. "No!" There, partially hidden behind a fallen bookcase, lay Heidi. I ran toward her.

"Maybe she's fainted. Heidi?"

No response.

Horror shot through my body at the dark pool of blood surrounding her head. She didn't appear to be breathing. Was she dead?

I pulled Molly close, trying to shield her from the gruesome sight, then released her. I knelt and pressed my fingers along Heidi's neck. Was there a faint pulse? *Please, God.*

"We need to call for an ambulance." I forced my voice to remain steady for Molly's sake. "And then the sheriff. Can you do that, sweetheart? The telephone's on the counter."

Molly made her way to the candlestick telephone. With shaking hands, she lifted the receiver and turned the crank.

"Number, please," came the tinny voice of the operator.

"We need an ambulance right away." Molly spoke barely above a whisper. "It's an emergency. We're at Elite Repeat on Main Street."

I couldn't tear my eyes away from Heidi's inert form. Sweet, kind Heidi, who'd always had a sunny greeting and a bargain for everyone who came into her shop. How could this have happened?

Had Heidi interrupted a burglary?

"Aunt Amanda?" Molly's voice broke through my thoughts. "Both the ambulance and the sheriff are on their way."

I nodded, pulling her close again. "You did well, Molly. Very well."

We stood there in shocked silence, waiting for help to arrive. James burst through the door moments later.

"Amanda? Molly? What's—" He stopped short, taking in the scene before him. His face hardened as he saw Heidi.

"Oh, h—," he muttered, then seemed to remember we were there. "Ladies, I'm going to need you to step outside. Deputy!" he called over his shoulder. "Secure the area!"

As he ushered us out, I caught one last glimpse of the smear of blood on the floor. My dear friend, who'd weathered the loss of her husband and built this little shop from nothing. Who'd faced every challenge with a smile and a kind word. She didn't deserve this. No one did.

Standing on the sidewalk in the growing morning light, watching the canvas-framed Model T ambulance swerve its way around the horse-drawn wagons, a resolve hardened within me. Whatever had happened here, whoever was responsible—they wouldn't get away with this.

Not in my town. Not to my friend.

***

A while later, I sat in Elite Repeat's back office, a forgotten cup of lukewarm tea trembling in my hands. Molly had already been questioned and released. I'd urged her to go home and rest after our ordeal, but she insisted on opening Mountain Melodies.

"I need to keep busy."

Outside the office came the thumps and scrapes of sheriff's deputies sifting through the shop. James was out of the building, combing the street and alleyway for clues.

Agent Frank Callaway, a man whose bulk seemed at odds with his gentle demeanor, settled into the creaky chair across from me. I hadn't met the agent before, but he seemed nice enough. James had explained he'd been brought in to help investigate the rash of vandalism against foreign-owned businesses.

"Now, Miss Parrish." Agent Callaway flipped open a small note-book. "Let's go over this one more time."

"Of course." I set down my cup. "Though I'm not sure how much help I'll be. It's all such a blur."

"Just tell me what you remember," Callaway encouraged.

"Well, my niece and I came by Elite Repeat to pick up some things she needed for her room. The door was unlocked, which I thought was odd for so early in the morning. I called out, but there was no answer. And then—" My voice caught in my throat.

Callaway's pencil paused. "Take your time, ma'am."

I took a deep breath. "I found her behind the counter. At first, I thought she'd fainted. But then I saw... I saw the blood." Tears pushed at the back of my throat. "That's when we called for an ambulance and the sheriff. I can't remember anything else. But as I told you earlier, I suspect Leon Danvers had something to do with it."

"The more likely explanation is that she attempted to stop a bur-glary in progress," Callaway said. "Our men are searching the shop now, trying to determine if anything of value was taken."

"I don't know how they'd be able to tell. The shop is always full of all kinds of merchandise, some valuable and some not so valuable."

"True, but so far the cash register drawer is still intact, and the safe has not been tampered with. And there are several clearly valuable items on display, pieces of jewelry and such, that were not taken."

I rubbed my forehead to dispel a growing headache. "If it wasn't a robbery, then I'm telling you, you need to look into Leon Danvers. He's been hounding poor Heidi to try to get her to sell her property. And while you're at it, look into Ernie Weiss's death, too. He and Heidi were next-door neighbors. He was getting the same treatment from Danvers, and his house was found in similar disarray." I slapped the desk in frustration. "I keep telling you this, over and over."

Callaway peered at me over his spectacles. "And *I* keep telling *you*, over and over, that we've looked into Danvers, and he's got a water-tight alibi. He was out of town on business the night of Mr. Weiss's ... accident."

"But what about last night? He wasn't out of town this week—I saw him at the Chamber of Commerce meeting with Oscar Bar-rington. You should look into Oscar, too. As I told James—Sheriff Holcomb—they were discussing how they had to get the new hotel built at any cost. What if 'any cost' meant Heidi's life?"

Agent Callaway sighed, his patience strained as much as mine. "I understand, Miss Parrish. But until we have some clear evidence pointing to—"

A young deputy burst into the room, his face flushed with excite-ment. "Agent Callaway! You need to see this!"

Callaway excused himself, leaving me alone with my thoughts, their muffled voices drifting back from the main shop area.

"It's definitely an ethnically motivated crime, sir," the young officer was saying. "Look at the wall!"

My curiosity got the better of me. I crept to the door and peered out. That's when I saw it—crude letters scrawled on the wall in what looked horribly like blood: "Go home, Kraut."

I might be sick. How had Molly and I missed that terrible message earlier? Perhaps the shop had been too dark, the message obscured in shadow until a rising sunbeam illuminated its horror.

Callaway's voice rumbled. "Looks like our perpetrator wanted to send a message. But why attack the woman and leave her for dead?"

"Maybe they just wanted to scare her, sir," the young officer suggested. "Things got out of hand."

I couldn't contain myself any longer. I stepped out of the office. "Excuse me, gentlemen, but are you confirming this wasn't a robbery, after all?"

Callaway turned, his expression softening. "Miss Parrish, you shouldn't be out here."

"I'm already out here," I snapped. "And I need to know what's going on. This is my friend we're talking about. And that message doesn't make any sense—Heidi isn't even German." In truth, I had no idea what Heidi's ethnic heritage was. It had been her late husband who'd bestowed her with the Teutonic-sounding Fischer. Was that enough to drive some folks to violence? My thoughts flicked to the Liberty League, and again to Leon and Oscar, who were both staunch members of that jingoist organization.

The agent grunted. "It appears the intruder was more interested in causing trouble than stealing. Unfortunately, things escalated."

Why wouldn't he listen to me *now*? "It was Danvers! Or Barrington! I know I'm right!"

Callaway pinched the bridge of his nose. "Look, Miss Parrish. Clearly the motive for the attack has been written on the wall."

How could he be so dense?

"Don't you see? Danvers was trying to scare her into selling her property and leaving town." The urge to stamp my foot was almost overwhelming. "Maybe he's even behind all this 'Go home, Kraut' business. I wouldn't put it past him. He might even be the leader of this anti-immigrant ring that's been vandalizing the town. Either him, or people he has working for him."

"Miss Parrish, get a hold of yourself," the agent ordered. "At this point, we have no reason to suspect Mr. Danvers of anything—not of attacking Mrs. Fischer, not of breaking and entering, not of writing that message. We need evidence."

This time I did stamp my foot. "But you have no suspects at all yet. What about the summer music camp? And the town's reputation? Agent Callaway, this crime wave could be disastrous for Timber Coulee on so many levels."

"Now, Miss Parrish—"

"No, you listen here." My voice rose. "We have young people coming from all over the country. Musicians, families. They need to know they'll be safe. And what about our townspeople? Heidi wasn't the only one with a foreign-sounding surname. Far from it."

The young officer shifted uncomfortably. "Ma'am, we're doing everything we can—"

"Well, do more," I snapped. "This isn't just about one terrible crime. It's about the soul of our town."

Callaway looked at me. "You're right, Miss Parrish. We'll increase patrols, especially around the camp. And we'll find who did this."

His mention of the camp sparked another remote possibility. One so unwelcome and preposterous, it shamed me to even think about, much less state out loud. But ... was it possible Heidi been having some kind of ... dalliance ... with Michael Tate? After all, he'd been visiting her early in the morning. And then Mrs. Abernathy saw them together in the hotel restaurant. And Carrie had admitted she hardly ever saw him these days. Perhaps they'd had a fight, or Heidi'd threatened to tell Carrie, or Carrie had found out and ....

My stomach churned at such devious suspicions about three people

I cared for deeply. What kind of a friend was I to think they were even capable of such dishonorable behavior? Firmly I thrust these thoughts out of my mind. The person responsible was Danvers. It had to be him.

I knew it in my bones.

"Are you feeling all right, Miss Parrish?" Agent Callaway looked at me with concern.

I nodded, drained. I'd said my piece. Time to let the professionals do their work, even if they weren't doing it to my satisfaction.

"Thank you. I... I should go, if you've got everything you need. My niece is alone in the music shop."

As I left, I couldn't shake the feeling that there was more to this than met the eye. The attack on Heidi, the ransacked shop, the hateful message, even Ernie's supposedly accidental death ... Something didn't add up. And if the sheriff's department couldn't figure it out, even with the help of this additional agent—well, perhaps it was up to me to uncover the truth.

Chapter Thirteen

The gentle tinkling of wind chimes filled the air as I watered the hanging baskets outside my shop. Amazed that my "black thumb" had kept the blooms alive this long, I didn't want to break my streak and tried to be dutiful about watering. The humble task also gave me time to think, and to pray, for Heidi and for everything else that seemed to be going haywire.

The cool morning breeze fluttered the petals, a stark contrast to the worry gnawing at my insides. I'd barely slept a wink, my dreams haunted by the mysterious note from Ernie's crate, as well as the attack on Heidi two days earlier. The hospital wasn't allowing her to have any visitors. Her condition was stable, a nurse had assured me when I telephoned, but she hadn't yet regained consciousness. Meanwhile, my prayer muscles were getting a lot of exercise.

The rumble of an approaching vehicle snapped me from my thoughts. The sheriff's Dodge pulled up, and my heart did a double turn as James stepped out, looking particularly sheriff-like in the morning light. The grim set of his jaw told me this wasn't a social call. What if he had bad news to share about Heidi? I steeled myself.

"G'morning, Amanda." He removed his hat. "Got a minute?"

I set down my watering can. "Of course. What's wrong?"

"I've just been to the hospital."

"Heidi." My throat constricted. "Is she—is she—"

"She's awake," he said, and my knees nearly buckled in relief. "But she doesn't remember anything about the attack."

"But she's awake," I repeated. That was the important thing. Maybe she would remember details over time, but for now, it was enough for me that she'd regained consciousness. "Can I go see her?"

"Not yet. Maybe tomorrow they'll allow visitors." James ran a hand over his blond head. "Also, we've had another vandalism incident. Up at the camp this time."

My stomach dropped. "The camp? But Molly's gone up there for rehearsal. Is she all right?"

"She's fine."

"And the campers? And Carrie and Michael?"

"Everybody's fine. No one was hurt. But there's been some vandalism. Looks like our intolerant group has struck again."

"Oh, no." I rushed to his side. "How bad is it?"

"They've painted some nasty slogans on the main lodge." His voice sounded tight with frustration. "And someone took a hammer to the piano in the rehearsal room."

"That's terrible!" How could anyone do such a thing? "What about Dieter? He's a foreigner. Did the vandalism have something to do with him?"

James's eyes narrowed. "Mr. Volkov is fine. He wasn't there when it happened."

"Thank goodness." I let out a breath I didn't realize I'd been holding. "But still, this is awful. First the Wasserman bakery, then Heidi's shop, now the camp. And all those young people up there ... What if someone had been hurt?"

James's grip tightened on his hat. "That's what worries me. These acts are escalating. We need to find out who's behind this before things get even more out of hand. Good thing we've got Agent Callaway to help us."

Callaway hadn't been any help when it came to solving Heidi's attack, but maybe he knew what he was doing in these vandalism cases.

"I take it Heidi still hasn't been able to identify her attacker," I probed.

James grimaced. "She doesn't remember anything, other than she'd come in early to work on some bookkeeping, thought she heard a noise in the shop, and went to investigate. The next thing she remembers is waking up in the hospital."

"So the message scrawled on the wall doesn't mean anything to her."

"No. But it could mean that our anti-German vandals are capable of violence. So far they've only damaged property, but ..."

He didn't need to say more. I wrung my hands, torn between concern for Molly and worry for Dieter. "Should I go up to the camp? Maybe I could help clean up, or..."

"It's probably best if you stay here for now." James's manner was brusquer than usual. "We're treating it as a crime scene. Besides, I'm sure Mr. Volkov is more than capable of taking care of himself, if need be."

There it was again—that slight edge to his voice when he mentioned Dieter. I raised an eyebrow. "Is everything all right?"

He softened a bit, offering me a small smile that didn't seem quite genuine. "Just worried about this case, that's all. Listen, Amanda, I know you want to help, but please promise me you'll be careful. Whoever's behind this, they're getting bolder. I couldn't bear it if..." He trailed off, his eyes meeting mine with an intensity that made my breath catch.

"I'll be careful," I promised. "But you know I can't just sit by and do nothing."

"I know. It's one of the things I lo– like about you." He cleared his throat. "Just... keep your eyes open, all right? And call me if you see or hear anything suspicious." He turned to leave.

"James?" He looked back, and I gave him a warm smile. "Thank you. For looking out for all of us."

He touched the brim of his hat, a ghost of a smile playing on his lips. "Always, Amanda. Always."

I watched him drive away, my emotions a jumbled mess. Concern for Molly and the camp, worry for Dieter, frustration at this senseless hatred... and underneath it all, gratitude for James's obvious care. He was a good sheriff, dedicated to his job.

But even the best law-enforcement official might need a little help now and then.

Especially with a web of suspicious circumstances as tangled and twisted as this one.

***

The next day, Heidi was allowed to have a few visitors. Having been warned by James to stay away from the camp for now, and with Molly safely back at work in the store, I headed to the hospital, a cheerful bouquet of wildflowers clutched in my hand. The sterile smell of disinfectant assaulted my nostrils in the corridor. My heels clicked against the polished floor, echoing in the quiet hallway. I paused outside Heidi's room and took a deep breath to steel myself before tapping on the door.

"Come in," Heidi's voice called, sounding more feeble than I'd ever heard it.

I pushed open the door, forcing a bright smile onto my face. "Heidi, dear! How are you feeling?"

She lay propped up in the hospital bed, her usually rosy cheeks pale against the stark white pillows. A nasty bruise bloomed across her left cheekbone and her head wore a bandage. Despite her condition, she managed a wan smile.

"Amanda, how lovely to see you." She gestured weakly to a chair beside her bed. "I'm as well as can be expected, I suppose."

I settled into the chair, placing the flowers on her bedside table. "I've been so worried about you. Do you... do you remember anything about what happened?"

Heidi's brow furrowed, as if thinking took great effort. "It's all so hazy. I was working in the office, and... and someone was out in the shop. Poking around, I think."

"Heidi." I leaned in, lowering my voice. "Was it Leon Danvers? Or Oscar Barrington? Did either of those men do this to you?"

Heidi's eyes widened, but then uncertainty clouded her features. "I... I don't know, Amanda. I don't think so, but..." She trailed off, shaking her head.

"What do you remember?" I pressed gently.

"It was dark." Heidi's fingers plucked at the blanket. "The figure was dressed all in black. I didn't see a face, but..." She paused, her forehead creasing with the effort of remembering. "He—or possibly she—seemed taller than Leon, and slimmer too. But beyond that, it's all a blur."

"It's all right, Heidi. Don't strain yourself. I'm just glad you're on the mend."

I tried to hide my disappointment that she wasn't able to point the finger at Leon. "Taller and slimmer" ruled out Carrie, too, as she was quite petite. But Michael possibly fit the description. Still, I refused to believe that dear man capable of such a dastardly deed. Could Oscar Barrington be the culprit? He wanted Heidi's property as much as Leon did. But that hardly seemed likely, since his goal was to boost the reputation of Timber Coulee, not to make it look like a center of criminal activity. Nonetheless, I made a mental note to discuss it with James.

We chatted for a while longer about inconsequential things—the weather, the latest town news—before a nurse came in to check Heidi's vital signs. Taking this as my cue to leave, I bid Heidi farewell and promised to visit again soon.

As I made my way towards the hospital exit, a familiar figure in the gift shop caught my eye. There stood Michael, perusing a display of flower arrangements. Curious, I paused to watch as he selected a bouquet of pink roses and carried them to the cashier.

"Get well soon," I heard him murmur to the cashier as she selected a card and wrapped the flowers.

I ducked out of sight as Michael exited the shop, not wanting him to spot me. He headed toward the staircase, and a number of questions swirled in my mind. Why would he be visiting Heidi without Carrie present? And why, if I were not mistaken, did he look so... so guilty?

The mystery surrounding Heidi's attack had just deepened, and a nagging doubt followed me around like Moxie begging to be fed. The truth was dangling out there somewhere, just beyond my reach.

Chapter Fourteen

The following Wednesday, Molly and I took the train to Spokane, a good ninety-minute ride through forested areas that gradually gave way to a flatter, sparser landscape.

Spokane was a bustling city, small in comparison to Chicago but a grand metropolis compared to Timber Coulee, with a mix of elegant Victorian mansions and more modest wooden homes lining its tree-shaded streets. The downtown area boasted impressive brick and stone buildings, including the dazzling new Davenport Hotel, while electric streetcars clanged along the main thoroughfares, ferrying residents and visitors alike. The Spokane River, with its dramatic falls, remained the heart of the city, powering sawmills and providing a scenic backdrop to the growing urban landscape.

Much as we might have liked to take our time seeing the sights, I hurried Molly along to Floyd Hendricks's repair shop. "We'll do the grand tour another time," I promised.

As she and I stepped into the familiar workshop, I breathed in the comforting scent of wood and varnish. Violin cases lined the walls, and tools were scattered across workbenches—a sight I'd grown accustomed to over years of working with the skilled specialist.

"Floyd?" I spotted the wispy white hair of my old friend hunched over his workbench.

He looked up, a warm smile spreading across his face as he peered at us over his half-moon glasses. "Amanda! What a pleasant surprise. And who's this young lady with you?"

"This is my niece, Molly Mulroney." I returned his smile. "Molly, meet Floyd Hendricks, the best luthier in the Northwest."

Floyd chuckled, setting down his tools. "You flatter me. Now, what brings you two in today? Another student's violin in need of some TLC?"

"Two violins in need of repair."

"Two, eh? Well, then, show me what you've got."

I signaled for Molly to go ahead. She lifted her violin case onto the counter and opened it. "Unfortunately, my violin was damaged on the train ride from Chicago," she told Floyd. "I didn't realize what had happened until I unpacked it."

He picked up the instrument and turned it over, frowning. "I have some bad news, I'm afraid," he said. "The sound board is cracked. Even if I'm able to repair it, it will never sound quite the same."

Tears welled in Molly's eyes. I grasped her hand.

"Will you at least try to fix it?" Her voice wobbled.

"I'll try." Floyd's gaze was sympathetic. "But I can't promise any-thing. If worse comes to worst, I'll write a certificate of damage so you can file a claim with the railroad. They're insured against this sort of thing and usually pretty good about paying."

"But it won't be the same as having my own violin back."

"No, it won't. But don't lose heart. I'll do my best." He sighed and looked at me. "You said you had two?"

I placed the other violin case on the counter, one I'd borrowed from the shop for the occasion, not wishing to lug a tomato crate onto the train. "Yes. We have another old violin that needs some repair work. I'm afraid it's in quite bad shape, but fixable, I think." I opened the case.

Floyd's eyes widened behind his spectacles. He let out a low whistle as he lifted the instrument, turning it over in his gnarled hands. "Now this... this looks like something special."

"It does?"

He examined it closely, running his fingers along the wood grain and peering inside. "Extraordinary craftsmanship. The wood choice, the varnish... You don't see instruments like this every day."

"Really?" Molly leaned in, intrigued.

A spark of curiosity ignited within me.

"It's secondhand," I explained, my mind racing with possibilities. "We got it from the estate of an—an old friend who passed away recently. I found it buried in an old fruit crate, of all things. I wonder what its story might be. There's no maker's mark on the inside, as far as I can tell."

"Yes, that is unusual." Floyd's fingers traced the curves of the violin, his touch almost reverent. "Even so it could be more significant than just an old violin. Much more." He paused, seeming to choose his words with care. "Of course, I'll need to examine it more closely to be sure."

The gleam in Floyd's eyes was like nothing I'd seen before. He was practically vibrating with excitement, though it was clear he was trying to contain it.

"More in what way?" I asked.

"I'd rather not go into details. Not until I'm sure."

"I see." I was a little annoyed at his caginess. "Well, you're the expert."

Floyd remained captivated by the violin. "Whoever owned it before knew quality. This instrument has tales to tell, no doubt about it. Amanda—" His voice was measured. "Would you mind terribly if I consulted with a colleague of mine in Boston? I'd like to send him some photographs of this instrument. Just to get a second opinion, you understand."

"Of course." Floyd's unusual behavior puzzled me. "I don't see why not. Is something wrong with it?"

Floyd choked out a sound caught between nervousness and glee. "Wrong? Oh no, nothing's wrong. It's just... well, let's not get ahead of ourselves. It could be something quite special, or it could be nothing at all. Best not to speculate until we know more."

"Will it take long to consult your colleague? I thought maybe you could fix it up for Molly to use at the music camp, especially if hers is out of commission for good."

He consulted a calendar on the wall. "Two weeks should do it. You can pick it up two weeks from today. Same time?"

I nodded, relief mixing with excitement. Two weeks meant she'd have it just in time for the grand finale concert on July twenty-ninth. "That would be perfect. Thank you. I can't wait to hear how it sounds once you've worked your magic."

Molly and I stepped out onto the street, but I couldn't shake the feeling that Floyd knew something he wasn't telling me. What was the story behind the violin? What stories could it tell? Where had it been? Who had played it? The possibilities were endless, and I found myself looking forward to unraveling its mysteries.

"Curiouser and curiouser," I muttered.

"*Alice in Wonderland.*" Molly interrupted my thoughts.

"What?"

"That's a quote from *Alice in Wonderland.*"

"Is it?" I mumbled, but my mind was far away. First Ernie's secret past, and now this mysterious violin. It seemed that Timber Coulee was determined to keep me on my toes this summer.

When we returned home, Molly headed up the mountain to rehearsal, while I returned to my book-organizing project. I picked up a weathered copy of the Bible, my heart aching as I recalled how Ernie had carried it faithfully to church each Sunday.

A yellowed piece of paper fluttered out, dancing in the air before settling on the carpet. I bent to retrieve it before Moxie pounced. It was a newspaper clipping, brittle with age.

The bold header "OBITUARY" caught my eye, followed by a name that made me pause.

Robert Allen Weiss.

"Weiss?" I frowned.

I skimmed the text, absorbing details. Robert Allen Weiss, born 1875, died 1898. Employed by the Blue Ribbon Grocery in Effingham, Illinois. A fine amateur clarinetist with the Effingham town band. Single man. Only son of Ernest and the late Camille Weiss.

The wedding portrait on Ernie's nightstand... My breath caught in my throat. "Could it be that our Ernie had not only a wife, but a son as well?" I whispered to Moxie.

I knew it couldn't have been Ernie who wrote that scrap of a note found with the old violin. The note had been written in an elegant hand, and Ernie's songwriting scrawl was as far from elegant as one could imagine. I'd thought it might possibly have been written by his wife. But maybe it wasn't Ernie *or* Camille who had some connection to the Northern Illinois Asylum.

It might have been Robert. Their son. Who lived in Illinois.

I sank into my armchair, the obituary trembling in my hands. My mind raced back to the old photograph Molly had found among Ernie's belongings, the one taken at the Chicago World's Fair. One of the young men pictured had been labeled "Luke" and the other "Bobby." Could "Bobby" have been this Robert? It seemed to make sense.

"Oh, Ernie." My heart ached anew for my old friend. "You never said a word about a son. Or a wife. About losing them both."

I gazed at the bookshelves, seeing them now in a new light. How many secrets had Ernie carried with him? How much sorrow had he hidden behind his twinkling eyes and ready smile?

His smile. I opened a desk drawer and retrieved the photograph of the two young men. Now that I looked more closely at "Bobby," I could see a resemblance to Ernie. Something about the eye-crinkling smile. If that were true, then clearly, Robert and Bobby were the same person.

But it was still Luke who caught my attention. He didn't look anything like Ernie, nor Robert. But he still reminded me of someone, if only slightly. I just couldn't remember who.

I folded the obituary and slipped it into the same drawer as the photograph and the shred of a note. I had a feeling that somehow they would add up to ... something. I just didn't know what.

Suddenly my stomach plummeted. I whipped open the drawer, pulled out the yellowed clipping, and stared at it.

Robert Allen Weiss. Robert Allen Weiss.

A new idea settled over me. The fruit crates had not been marked with the word "raw." They were marked with initials. R. A. W. They'd contained the personal effects of Robert A. Weiss.

All the musical scores. The clarinet. The piccolo. The old violin. The strange note.

They'd all belonged to Robert.

In spite of the late hour, I flew over to the shop to telephone James with news of my discovery. I cranked the telephone handle and tapped my foot, waiting for the operator. "Number, please?" came the familiar nasal twang. I asked for James, praying he was in his office and not out checking speed limits. The new law restricting automobiles to fifteen miles per hour in town was keeping him busy.

"Those crates in the shed weren't Ernie's," I blurted when he came on the line. "They belonged to Robert."

James's voice sounded sleepy. "Who's Robert?"

"Ernie's son."

"Ernie had a son?"

It dawned on me that James was not yet privy to any of the information I was hurling at him. Only I had seen the obituary thus far. I backed up and filled him in.

"Ernie had a son named Robert. Robert Allen Weiss. I figure it's the same young man who was labeled "Bobby" in that photograph Molly found. The dates seem right. He would have been about eighteen years old when that photograph was taken at the Chicago World's Fair." I stopped to take a breath. "The obituary said Robert died in Effingham, Illinois, in 1898. At the time he was working in a grocery. The obit also claimed he was an amateur clarinetist, so the clarinet in the box must have been his. My hunch is that after his death, somebody—possibly the grocer he worked for—packed up his belongings and shipped them to Ernie, his next of kin. And that Ernie, in his grief, stuffed it all in the shed to look through later. Only later never came." A wave of sadness socked me in the gut. My voice cracked. "Maybe he forgot about it, or maybe he just couldn't face—" Another surge of compassion silenced my tongue.

"Should I come over there?" Concern laced James's words.

I pulled myself together. "No need. I'm just a little wistful, that's all, remembering that I did the same thing when my parents died. It took me forever to work up the courage to go through their belongings. And even then, it was one of the hardest things I'd ever done." I glanced at the clock. "It's getting late. We'll talk tomorrow."

"All right," James said. "As always, I'm here if you need me."

"Thanks, James. Good night."

The receiver clicked. This man couldn't suspect how much his calm presence and reassuring attitude made me feel safe and protected, even at a distance. *He's an absolute godsend, and I really ought to tell him how much he means to me. Maybe I will.*

Someday.

Chapter Fifteen

On Thursday evening, I was doing some more work, puzzling out possible meanings from Ernie's song lyrics, when my eyes flicked to the grandfather clock in the hall. Goodness, it *was* getting late. High time for Molly to be returning from rehearsal. I made my way to the kitchen to heat water for our nightly tea.

The hour grew later. The grandfather clock chimed ten, each resonant gong setting my nerves further on edge. I paced the living room, the worn rug muffling my footsteps, pausing now and then to peer out the window into the inky darkness. The scent of cooling chamomile tea, long forgotten on the side table, mingled with the lingering aroma of beeswax from a dwindling candle.

"Where is that girl?" I twisted a handkerchief between my fingers. Molly should have been home by now. Camp Harmony wasn't that far, even accounting for a longer-than-normal rehearsal. What if the wagon had broken an axle or veered into a ditch on its way down the mountain? Or if she'd defied my wishes and ridden her bicycle . . .

Dread jolted through my veins as unwelcome thoughts crept in. Heidi's attacker was still at large. What if... No. I shook my head, banishing the dark imaginings. But still, the worry gnawed at me like a persistent mouse.

Minutes ticked by and worry gave way to frustration, then anger. "I bet she's ridden that blasted bicycle down the mountain in the dark." My reflection scowled back at me from the window pane. "After she promised she wouldn't! Of all the reckless, foolhardy—"

The distant rumble of an engine cut through my rant. Headlights swept across the front yard, illuminating the flowerbeds for a brief moment before going dark. I rushed to the door and yanked it open just as Molly was about to knock.

"Molly Mulroney!" I began, ready to unleash my pent-up worry and frustration. But the words died on my lips as I took in the scene before me.

Molly stood on the porch, looking sheepish but unharmed. Behind her, shifting awkwardly from foot to foot, was a lanky young man with a mop of unruly dark hair and Rose MacTavish's violin case clutched to his skinny chest like a shield. It took me a moment to recognize him as Molly's trumpeter friend from the Fourth of July picnic.

"I'm so sorry I'm late, Aunt Amanda," Molly said. "The rehearsal ran long, and then I got to talking to Clarence and missed the wagon to town, and you'd warned me not to ride my bicycle after dark, and—"

"And I offered to drive Miss Mulroney home," the young man interjected, his voice cracking slightly on 'Miss'. He cleared his throat and tried again. "I hope that was all right, ma'am. I borrowed my uncle's Model T. I have my license and everything!"

The tension drained from my shoulders, replaced by a bubbling sense of amusement. "I see." I struggled to keep a straight face. "And you are...?"

The boy looked startled, as if just remembering his manners. "Oh! Uh, Clarence Butterworth, ma'am. I play the trumpet. At the camp, I mean. Not professionally or anything. Yet. I mean—"

"Clarence is very talented," Molly interrupted, throwing him a lifeline. "He has a beautiful tone."

Clarence's face flushed a deep red visible even in the dim porch light. "Gosh, thanks, Miss Mulroney."

I bit the inside of my cheek to keep from grinning. "Well, Mr. Butterworth, thank you for seeing Molly home safely. Would you like to come in for some tea or—"

"Oh, no, thank you, ma'am!" Clarence blurted, already backing toward the Model T. "I should get back to the camp. It's late. I mean, not too late. Just, you know, late enough." He turned to Molly, his eyes wide. "I could... that is if you wanted... maybe I could pick you up for the next rehearsal? To save you the bicycle ride?"

Molly's smile was warm. "That would be lovely, Clarence. Thank you."

The poor boy looked like he might faint from happiness. "Swell! I mean, great. I'll, uh, see you then. Goodnight, Miss Mulroney. Ma'am. Oh, here." He thrust the violin case at Molly. Then, with a jerky bow, he retreated to the automobile.

The Model T puttered away, and I turned to Molly, who was watching it disappear down the lane with a bemused expression.

"Well." I ushered her inside. "It seems I owe you an apology. I'm afraid I jumped to conclusions and thought you'd disobeyed me about the bicycle."

Molly hung up her coat. "You don't need to apologize. I'm sorry I worried you. I should have telephoned, but Clarence and I got lost in conversation and I lost track of time and ... and I just didn't think."

I waved away her explanation, suddenly feeling every one of my years. "It's all right, dear. I'm just glad you're home safe." I paused, a mischievous smile tugging at my lips. "So... Clarence seems nice."

Molly groaned, but I caught the hint of a blush on her cheeks. "Aunt Amanda, don't start. He's just a friend. A very kind, if somewhat awkward, friend."

"Mmhmm." I headed to the kitchen to pour some iced tea. "A friend who blushes redder than a tomato every time you so much as look at him."

"Oh, stop it." Molly laughed, following me. "You're impossible."

We settled in with our tea, the earlier tension melting away like morning mist. "You know, for all your talk of being modern, I do believe you've managed to acquire yourself a good old-fashioned admirer."

Molly rolled her eyes, but her smile was fond. "Well, I suppose even us modern girls can appreciate a gentleman now and then. Especially one who can rescue a damsel stranded on a mountain."

We sipped our tea together, the warm glow of the kitchen lamps casting everything in a cozy light. For a moment, the worries of unsolved murders and mysterious violins faded into the background, overshadowed by the simple joy of family, safety, and the promise of young love—however awkward it might be.

***

The shop was warm and fragrant with the scent of honeysuckle from the open doorway as Molly and I worked side-by-side, dusting shelves. I kept glancing at her. She'd been uncharacteristically quiet this morning.

"All right, out with it," I said at last. "What's on your mind?"

Molly looked up, her brown eyes troubled. "Aunt Amanda, I... I need to talk to you about Mr. Volkov."

A flutter let loose in my chest at the mention of his name. "Oh? What about him?"

Molly took a deep breath. "I'm worried. There's something... off about him."

I set down my dust rag. "What do you mean, 'off'?"

"Well, it's little things." Molly's words tumbled out in a rush. "The way he watches us when we're not playing, like he's searching for something. And sometimes, when he thinks no one's looking, his accent slips."

A derisive cackle escaped my lips, though it sounded forced even to my own ears. "Oh, Molly. You've been reading too many mystery novels. Dieter is just dedicated to his craft. And as for his accent, well, he's probably picking up some American inflections."

Molly shook her head, her jaw set. "It's more than that. Yesterday, I overheard him in the office, muttering to himself. At first, I didn't even think it was him. No trace of an accent at all."

A twinge of unease crept in, but I pushed it aside. "That's impossible. Perhaps you misheard. I'm sure there's a perfectly reasonable explanation."

"I didn't mishear." Her volume ticked up a notch. "And he's so strict and demanding, especially with us violins. It's like he cares more about perfection than the actual music. None of us are professionals, and the campers are actually getting scared of him."

I shot to my feet, nearly knocking over a snare drum. "Now, that's enough, Molly. Dieter is a respected musician and a gentleman. I won't have you spreading gossip and wild theories about him."

Molly's eyes widened, hurt flashing across her face. "But I'm just trying to—"

"I said enough." Immediately, I regretted my tone, but pride kept me from apologizing. "Dieter has been nothing but kind and gracious to us both. I'm sure you're just misinterpreting things."

Molly rose, anger blazing in her eyes. "Or maybe you're the one misinterpreting things," she muttered. "You're so caught up in his charm that you can't see what's right in front of you."

My cheeks flushed with anger and embarrassment. "Young lady, that is quite enough. I think you should go home and practice for the concert. We'll discuss this no further."

Molly stared at me for a long moment, her eyes glittering with unshed tears. Then, without another word, she left the shop, her footsteps heavy on the plank floor.

After the door slammed behind her, I sank back against the counter, my hands shaking as I resumed dusting a shelf I'd already dusted.

"Oh, Dieter," I murmured, trying to summon the warmth I'd felt at our last meeting. But all I could think of was the hurt in Molly's eyes and the nagging doubt her words had planted in my mind.

I gave myself a stern talking-to. Molly was just being overprotective, that's all. She didn't know Dieter like I did. And yet... as I stood there in the fading afternoon light, I couldn't quite shake the feeling that maybe, just maybe, there was more to Dieter Volkov than met the eye.

Chapter Sixteen

A day later, Heidi was released from the hospital. James gave her a lift home in the Dodge. I went to visit her and reassure myself that she was making a good recovery.

The scent of rose petals filled Heidi's cozy living room as I settled into an overstuffed armchair. Heidi, looking much better than when I'd last seen her in the hospital, sat across from me, a cheerful patchwork quilt draped over her lap.

"It's so good to see you up and about." I gave my friend a warm smile.

Heidi's eyes twinkled. "It feels wonderful to be home. And I can't wait to reopen Elite Repeat. Just waiting on the doctor's final approval."

"That's marvelous news." I hesitated before asking, "Have you... remembered anything else about the attack?"

She looked toward the window, her fingers absently tracing the quilt's patterns. "Not much, I'm afraid. It's still mostly a blur. But..." She paused, her brow furrowing. "I do have this vague memory. A man's voice, muttering something as he ransacked the store."

I leaned forward, my heart quickening. "What did he say?"

"It was odd," Heidi mused. "He had a deep voice, and he kept saying things like, 'Where are you, my love? I can't live without you.'

Over and over, as if he were playing hide-and-seek with someone."

That description didn't sound at all like Leon Danvers or Oscar Barrington. "'My love'? Have you been carrying on some grand love affair you haven't told me about?" I teased.

Amusement tugged at her lips. "You've seen the line-up of available bachelors in Timber Coulee. What do you think?"

We shared a giggle. Then a sudden vision of Michael Tate buying flowers flashed across my mind, and I grew serious. "So it was definitely a man, then. Not a boy. And not a woman."

"Yes, a man. But not a voice I recognized."

A wave of relief washed over me. So the intruder couldn't have been Michael. Or Carrie, for that matter. Heidi would have recognized Michael's voice. And Carrie... well. A giggle escaped my throat.

"What's so funny?"

"Believe it or not, I feared for a moment it might have been Carrie Tate."

Disbelief bloomed across Heidi's face. "Carrie Tate? That sweet little thing? Why on earth would you think she'd do something like that?"

Embarrassment heated my face. I hadn't meant to blurt out my private suspicions, but now that I had, I owed Heidi an explanation.

"Oh, Heidi." I sighed. "I'm ashamed to admit it, but... well, I had this brief, terrible suspicion that you and Michael might have been... involved."

"Involved?" The puzzled look on her face was replaced by under-standing. Her cheeks grew scarlet. "Oh! Oh, my goodness, Amanda!"

I hurried on, desperate to explain. "It's just that you were seen together a few times, just the two of you. Michael leaving Elite Repeat early one morning, Mrs. Abernathy spotting you having lunch at the hotel, and I saw him buying flowers at the hospital. And Carrie mentioned rarely seeing her husband during camp season. I let my imagination run wild, and I'm so sorry."

To my surprise, Heidi burst out laughing. "Oh, Amanda, you dear thing. Is that what's been worrying you?"

I nodded, feeling foolish.

She patted my hand. "Michael was simply helping me as my banker. We've been working on a legal and financial strategy to thwart Leon Danvers's efforts to get my property. And I think we've succeeded!"

Relief and joy flooded through me. "Oh, Heidi, that's wonderful news! And I'm so sorry for even entertaining such thoughts about you and Michael."

"Nonsense." Heidi's eyes twinkled. "In a small town like ours, it's only natural for imaginations to run wild sometimes. I'm just glad we cleared it up."

I stood and moved to Heidi's chair, enveloping her in a warm embrace. "Me too, dear friend. Me too."

The last of my worries about Heidi and Michael melted away. But a new concern took its place—who was the man in Heidi's shop, and what was he so desperate to find there?

***

A few days before the grand finale concert, I returned to Spokane by myself to pick up the violins, leaving Mountain Melodies in Molly's capable hands. The morning after our quarrel, after a good night's sleep, we'd apologized to each other for our harsh words. But I still sensed that Dieter Volkov was a topic of conversation best avoided for the time being. I hoped that she would come to see his good qualities as I did, before both of them left Timber Coulee at the end of the summer, leaving me alone once more—a looming event that didn't bear thinking about.

I so rarely visited Spokane, especially during the busy summer months, that I'd tried to cram too many errands into my trip. Unfortunately, I'd chosen one of the hottest days of the year and, in desperate need of rest and refreshment, I'd stopped for what I hoped would be a quick lunch, but the dining room at the Crescent department store was crowded and service was slow. By the time I'd finished my meal and settled the bill, I had just enough time to pick up the violins at Floyd's and head to the station to catch my train. If I missed it, I'd have to wait for the next one, which would get me back to Timber Coulee quite late.

I rushed into Floyd Hendricks's repair shop, heart racing.

"Is Mr. Hendricks here?" I rasped to the clerk behind the counter.

"No," said the bespectacled young man. "I'm afraid Mr. Hendricks has gone to a meeting. Is there something I can do for you?"

"I'm here to pick up two violins," I told him. "They should be under the name Amanda Parrish. Or possibly Molly Mulroney and Amanda Parrish."

The clerk disappeared into the back room. I drummed my fingers on the counter, willing him to hurry. After what felt like an eternity, he returned with only one case.

"I've got the Mulroney violin here, but I can't seem to find the Parrish one." He set the case on the counter and pushed up his spectacles.

My stomach dropped. "You can't find it? But Mr. Hendricks said they'd both be ready today. It's very important."

The clerk bit his lip, looking flustered. "Let me take another look."

He hurried to the back of the shop. I shifted from foot to foot, anxiety building with each passing second. As I waited, I opened

Molly's case, lifted the violin and bow, and played a quick passage to check the work Floyd had done. If anyone could fix it, he could.

Sadly, it was apparent that even he couldn't fix the problem. Molly's violin sounded all wrong. With the sound board cracked, it would never sound right again. I returned it gently to the case, as though placing it in a coffin, and clicked the lid shut.

At last, the clerk emerged, carrying the second violin case.

"Found it!" he announced, relief evident in his voice. "That's strange, though. I found it locked up in Mr. Hendricks's office. He doesn't usually keep the instruments back there."

"Well, thank goodness you found it." I took a quick peek at Ernie's violin. It looked like a new instrument, gleaming and golden. I plucked a string. Satisfied, I gathered both cases. Molly might get good use of it for the rest of the summer. Even if she chose not to play it, it would fetch a nice price at retail, for the right buyer.

I thanked the clerk for his help. "What do I owe you?"

"Mr. Hendricks will mail you an invoice." Another push of the spectacles. "But ... it might be better if you wait for him to return. Just to make sure it's ready to go."

"I don't have time to wait. I have to catch my train."

I caught sight of the clerk's bemused expression. He seemed puzzled about something, but I was too preoccupied with my tardiness to dwell on it. I rushed out the door.

Once outside, I took a deep breath, relieved to have both violins safely in hand. Why had Ernie's violin been in Floyd's office, instead of where the clerk expected to find it? Did that mean he hadn't quite finished working on it? Perhaps I should have waited for confirmation from Floyd himself that it was ready to be picked up. But he'd said the repair would take two weeks, and he was always a man of his word. I pushed these thoughts aside. I had a ninety-minute train ride ahead of me to do all the thinking I needed to.

Top of the list, of even greater importance than Floyd's business practices, was how to console Molly when she learned her beloved instrument would never sound the same again.

Chapter Seventeen

Molly sat cross-legged on the floor of the living room, her brow wrinkled in concentration as she ran a soft cloth along the curves of her instrument.

"I'm so sad that Mr. Hendricks couldn't fix it." Her words were tinged with disappointment. "Not his fault, of course. But I've had this violin since I was twelve. It feels like losing a friend."

I settled into my favorite armchair, the familiar creak of its springs a comforting sound. "I know, sweetie. But these things happen. At least Rose was kind enough to lend you hers."

Molly nodded. "Hers is a nice violin. Not quite like mine, but..." She trailed off, her eyes drifting to the third violin case propped against the bookshelf.

I followed her gaze, a small smile tugging at my lips. "You know, you're welcome to use Ernie's—or should I say Robert's—violin for the concert, if you'd prefer. I noticed how taken you were with its tone when you tried it out."

Molly's eyes lit up for a moment, but then she shook her head. "Oh, I couldn't. It's... well, it's remarkable, isn't it? The way it sings, even after all these years in storage. I've never heard anything quite like it. But I've been rehearsing with Rose's all season. Switching now might throw me off."

I leaned forward, the scent of lemon polish and rosin filling my nostrils. "Are you sure? There's still time to get used to it. And you seemed so natural with it."

Molly bit her lip, clearly tempted. "It did feel... right, somehow. Like it was made for my hands." She shook her head again, more firmly this time. "But no, I'd better stick with Rose's. I wouldn't want to risk messing up the performance. Maybe next time?"

I tried to hide my disappointment. Something about that old violin called to me, as if it held secrets just waiting to be uncovered. But Molly was right to be cautious. "Of course, dear. Whatever makes you most comfortable. After all, the music is what matters, not the instrument that makes it."

Molly's relief was evident in the relaxation of her shoulders. "Exactly. Though..." She cast one last, longing look at Robert's violin. "Maybe I could practice with it a bit? Just to see?"

"I think that can be arranged. In the meantime, if you think you won't be using your old violin, what would you think if we gave it away?"

"I don't see why not. I won't be playing it anymore."

"You see, sometimes children come to camp without instruments of their own. In fact, there's a local boy there now, Timothy Hawkins, who's in need of a violin. I'd love to give him yours, if you're willing."

"Sure, if you think he'd like it. I'd feel better about the whole situation if someone could still get some use out of it, even though it's not perfect. Then it wouldn't be a total loss."

"Excellent. Thank you." I gave her shoulders a squeeze. "Now, how about some tea before you get back to your scales?"

***

The following afternoon after we closed the shop, I rode the wagon up to the camp with Molly's repaired violin, picturing young Timothy's eager face when I gave it to him. Molly chose not to ride with me, but instead to take her bicycle.

When the wagoneer helped me down at Camp Harmony, the afternoon sun filtered through the pines, casting cool shadows across the gravel drive. A cacophony of musical instruments drifted from various cabins—someone practicing scales on a clarinet, an enthusiastic if slightly off-key trombone, the deep resonance of a cello.

I retrieved Molly's violin from the wagon bed and made my way to the camp office. "Amanda!" Carrie looked up from her desk, her reading glasses perched on the end of her nose. "What brings you up the mountain?"

"I brought a violin for Timothy Hawkins." I held up the case. "Dieter mentioned the boy needed one. It's not in great shape, but it's better than nothing for a camper."

Carrie's eyebrow lifted. "Timothy Hawkins? But he brought his own violin. A lovely instrument—it's been in his family for generations. His grandmother was quite insistent about that when she enrolled him."

"Are you sure?" The violin case felt heavy in my hands. "Dieter specifically told me Timothy had no instrument of his own."

"I'm quite certain." Carrie riffled through some papers on her desk and pulled out a file. "Yes, here it is. 'Camper will provide own instrument.' It's right here on his registration form."

I sank into a chair. "I don't understand. But why would Dieter tell me...?"

"Perhaps he was thinking of another student?" Carrie always assumed the best of people.

"Perhaps." But something felt off. Why had Dieter been so interested in whether I had violins for sale? And why make up a story about Timothy? Unless he had, indeed, mistaken the boy for someone else.

"Well, since you've brought it all this way, we could always add it to our collection of camp instruments," Carrie offered. "We often have students who need to borrow one."

"Yes, of course." I handed over the case, trying to shake off my unease. "That would be perfect." I eyed the registration form on the desk. "Carrie, I'm interested in Dieter's background, and I don't remember whether he played with the Cleveland orchestra, or the one in Cincinnati. Would you mind if I took a look at his application?"

"I'm pretty sure it was Cleveland." She tipped her head. "Why? Does it matter?"

"I just thought ... you know, the board ought to know these things. In case we want to hire him again."

A sly smile spread across Carrie's face. "You like him, don't you."

My face heated. "From what I've heard, I think he's quite a competent director and musician, if somewhat demanding on the campers."

She wasn't buying it. "Mhmm. Well, I know for a fact that he thinks quite highly of you, too." Pleasure melted through my chest like warm honey. But before I could ask how she could know such a thing *for a fact*, she said, "As it happens, he didn't fill out an application."

That was a surprise. "He didn't?"

She lifted her hands in a gesture of futility. "Contrary to our normal practice, we hired him out of desperation, on the strength of the agent's recommendation."

"I see. Well, perhaps I could talk to him, then, since I'm here."

"I'm afraid he's tied up in rehearsal at the moment. But of course, you're welcome to wait."

"No matter," I said. "It's not a big deal. I'll be seeing him soon, anyway." He'd promised to pick me up early and take me to dinner before the big concert.

But as I rode the wagon back down the mountain, the conversation nagged at me like a mosquito bite. First the conflicting stories about which orchestra he'd played with, and now the falsehood—or was it a simple mistake?—about Timothy Hawkins needing a violin. Was there anything else Dieter Volkov had been less than candid about?

The sun was setting as I reached town, painting the sky in brilliant shades of orange and pink. But all I could think about as I walked down Main Street was the growing list of questions surrounding our mysterious maestro.

A burst of muffled laughter drew my attention to Timber Coulee's sole alleyway, the narrow passage between Henderson's Hardware and the Majestic Theater.

Five or six boys huddled there, heads bent together in conspiratorial fashion. I recognized most of them—the Mulligan twins, Tommy Peterson, and front and center, Rodney Barrington, Oscar and Martha's only son. They were passing something between them that looked suspiciously like a paint can. My mind flew to the recent vandalism incidents. But I knew these to be good boys. Surely they weren't up to no good. Even so ...

"Good evening, boys." I kept my voice deliberately casual.

They jumped like spooked rabbits. Rodney quickly shoved whatever he was holding behind his back. The others shuffled their feet, suddenly fascinated by their shoelaces.

"Oh! Hello, Miss Parrish." Rodney's voice cracked on the greeting. He still hadn't quite mastered his adult voice. "Nice out, isn't it?"

"Indeed." I studied their guilty faces. "What brings you all out this fine evening?"

"Boy Scouts!" Tommy blurted. The Mulligan twins elbowed him simultaneously.

"Really?" I shifted my handbag. "I wasn't aware the Boy Scouts met on Thursdays."

"Special meeting," Rodney said smoothly. His mother's gift of gab must have been hereditary. "We're working on our... our..."

"Citizenship badge," one of the twins supplied.

"Yes, exactly." Rodney's smile was too bright. "Citizenship. Very important stuff."

"How interesting." I looked from one to the other. "And what sort of citizenship activities require paint?"

The boys exchanged panicked glances.

"We're... painting a fence!" Tommy said. "For widow Johnson!"

"For the badge," Rodney added quickly. "Community service and all that."

I raised an eyebrow. "That's very thoughtful. Though I could have sworn I saw Mrs. Johnson's fence being painted just last week by her nephew."

More shuffling. More guilty looks.

"Well, we should get going," Rodney announced. "Don't want to be late for our... meeting."

The boys began edging away, still trying to keep whatever they were carrying hidden from view.

"Just a moment." My voice stopped them. "You know, it occurs to me that if you boys need a project for your citizenship badge, Mountain Melodies could use a fresh coat of paint. In broad daylight, of course. With proper supervision."

Their faces went pale.

"Thanks, Miss Parrish, but we've got it covered," Rodney mumbled. "Come on, fellows."

They hurried off, heads down, whispering furiously among themselves. I watched them go, noting which direction they took. Perhaps I should mention this encounter to James. After all, there had been that rash of vandalism lately...

I made a mental note to keep a closer eye on Rodney Barrington and his friends. Something told me their "Boy Scout meeting" had nothing to do with earning badges.

Unless, of course, there was a badge for suspicious behavior. In that case, they'd just earned it with flying colors.

Chapter Eighteen

Before returning home, I stopped in at the store to telephone James with my suspicions about the boys.

"I don't want to get them into trouble if they truly are innocent," I said. "But something was up. With all the vandalism that's going on around town, I think it's worth checking out."

"Will do. Thanks, Amanda."

With Molly still at rehearsal, I filled the quiet evening by tackling a project I'd started working on. The old wooden grocery crates from Ernie's place, once destined for the scrap heap, now gleamed with fresh white paint, artfully arranged as bookshelves against my living room wall. I stepped back, hands on my hips, and surveyed my handiwork with satisfaction. It gave me pleasure to think how pleased Ernie would have been to see his old crates put to such good use.

"Well, Ernie," I murmured, "I think we've done you proud."

A twinge of sorrow pinched at my heart as I thought of my old friend. The town wasn't the same without Ernie's cheerful whistling as he tinkered in his workshop or his animated stories of the good old days.

Satisfied with how the bookcase had turned out, I turned to the stacks of books waiting to be shelved and soon became absorbed in the project. Ernie had wide-ranging literary tastes, and leafing through the volumes slowed my progress in getting them on the shelves.

Suddenly my fingers touched a worn leather cover, then recoiled as if singed on a hot stove. It was Ernie's songwriting journal, which I'd steered clear of since the night when, delirious with sleeplessness, I'd suspected it of containing coded messages. My face burned at the memory. What a silly goose I was! Why, there was nothing in it but a bunch of song lyrics and chords. Which I'd have to look at sooner or later, if I was to keep my promise to arrange a song for the Mountain Meadowlarks to sing.

Gingerly, I opened the cover and peeked inside.

Yep, my notes were still there. I didn't *want* Ernie's songs to contain messages. But I couldn't unsee what I had seen. They were no longer just songs to me. They were codes. And it was my duty to figure them out.

There was nothing for it but to pick up my pad and pencil and get back to work.

Two hours later, a knock at the door startled me out of my decoding operation. I shoved the notebook under a sofa pillow and opened the door to find Agent Callaway's broad frame filling the doorway. I looked past him, expecting to see James, but he'd come alone.

"Good evening, Miss Parrish." The agent removed his hat. "Do you have a moment?"

"Of course. What brings you by?"

He gestured toward the small seating area near the window. "I have some news about the vandalism cases."

My heart quickened as I settled onto the sofa. The agent took a seat on my favorite armchair. Moxie, ever curious, hopped onto the windowsill to observe our conversation.

"Thanks to you, we've identified the culprits behind the ethnically motivated incidents," Callaway began, his voice low. "It's a group of local high school boys. The ones you had suspicions about."

"Oh, dear." I'd so hoped I'd been mistaken. "But why?"

Callaway rubbed his forehead. "It seems they were acting out of misguided fear. Their fathers work for Goldwood Corporation, and there's been talk of bringing in immigrant workers. The boys thought if they stirred up enough fear and prejudice against people from other countries, it might prevent that from happening."

"Good heavens," I murmured, thinking of the damage they'd caused.

"All of the boys' parents are being notified as we speak. Rodney Barrington appears to be the ringleader."

"The one born with a silver spoon in his mouth. Oscar and Martha must be mortified. But it does kind of make sense. Oscar's a staunch member of the Liberty League, and Rodney may have picked up certain anti-foreigner attitudes at home."

"All true," Callaway confirmed. "Rodney is the culprit behind the poison-pen letter sent to you and other members of the camp board, demanding that Stuart von Bauer be disinvited. The rest of the boys have confessed to the vandalism at the camp and other locations around town. They're facing consequences, of course, but given their age and the nature of the crimes, it'll likely be community service and probation."

"I see." I turned this information over in my mind. "But what about that terrible attack on Heidi? And that despicable message on her wall?" *And the secret coded messages in Ernie Weiss's notebook?* I thought but didn't say, lest he take me for a lunatic.

Callaway's expression turned grave. "That's the thing, Miss Parrish. The boys insist they had nothing to do with the attack on Mrs. Fischer or the slur written in her shop. They seemed genuinely shocked when I told them about it."

That seemed consistent with what Heidi had told me. She'd remembered a lone attacker, not a gang of boys. Although the description "taller and slimmer than Leon" could possibly apply to the gangly Rodney. Even so, it seemed unlikely the boy would have acted alone.

"So if it wasn't them..."

"Then we're still looking for whoever attacked Mrs. Fischer," Callaway finished. "It seems we may be dealing with two separate issues here. The vandalism at Elite Repeat appears to be what we call a copycat crime, an offense inspired by a previous crime that has received a lot of attention."

"I know what a copycat crime is," I snapped.

"I'm sure you do." I'd barely opened my mouth when he added, "And before you say it, Leon Danvers didn't do it. Witnesses have corroborated that he was in Spokane on the night of the attack, just as he was in Missoula on the night Ernie died. The man travels a great deal on business."

More's the pity. I would have liked to see the smarmy Leon Danvers get his due. But not for a crime he didn't commit. I didn't dislike him *that* much.

Various scenarios clicked through my mind. Whoever attacked Heidi must have truly meant what they wrote, or else they wanted to direct blame to the bigots by scrawling that terrible message on the wall. It was a brilliant plan that almost worked. But if the attacker didn't ransack the shop to steal things or to punish Heidi for her German surname . . . then what *did* he want?

"Will you be heading back to Boise now that the vandalism situation has been resolved?"

"Soon. Still a few loose ends to tie up first. And I think I might stick around for that big concert everyone keeps talking about, since it's only a few days away."

"I hope you will." Fancy the gruff Federal agent being a music lover.

"It was nice working with you, Miss Parrish."

I liked the way he said "working with." It made me feel like a colleague in the crime-solving sphere.

"Goodbye. And thank you for telling me about Rodney and his gang. I'm glad I could help, and I appreciate being kept in the loop."

Callaway stood to leave, but paused. "Miss Parrish, I know you have a... keen interest in these matters. But please, leave the investigating to us professionals. We don't want anyone else getting hurt."

I gave him a smile that was meant to be reassuring, even while formulating new theories. "Of course. You can count on me to stay out of trouble."

He grunted, as if he didn't believe me. Suddenly I was consumed by an overwhelming impulse to show the detective what I'd found in Ernie's notebook. He might be impressed by my code-cracking prowess. On the other hand, he might tell me I was imagining things. Either outcome would be better than living with the terrible uncertainty.

"Agent Callaway," I said, before he could leave. "There's something else." I pulled Ernie's notebook out from under the sofa pillow. "I've been looking through Ernie's songs, and... well, look at this one." I pointed to a page. "See how the train directions keep changing, and the signal colors—"

"Miss Parrish." He took the notebook, glanced at it, and handed it back to me. "Between the vandalism and Mrs. Fischer's attack, we have our hands full. I don't have time to analyze an amateur songwriter's creative process."

"But look here." I flipped to the counting song. "See how the second version changes? It's full of watchers and agents and—"

"Clearly a creative man exploring different themes." Callaway snatched the notebook back and tucked it under his arm. "Though I suppose I should take this with me. Just to be thorough."

Something in his tone made me hesitate. But what choice did I have? I'd already copied down the most suspicious parts in my own notebook.

"Of course," I said. "Just... please return it to me when you're done. I'll need it back."

"Naturally." He touched the brim of his hat. "Good evening, Miss Parrish."

As I watched him walk away, I couldn't shake the feeling I'd just made either a very good decision or a very bad one.

***

On the day of the grand finale concert, it was hard to keep my mind on my work due to nervous anticipation. I'd given Molly the day off to prepare. Dieter had promised to pick me up for an early dinner before the concert. I'd decided to wear the white lawn dress he'd admired on the Fourth of July, and had spent most of the previous evening pressing its many ruffles. As I entered figures into the ledger, I rehearsed how I'd ask Dieter about the seeming inconsistencies in his stories. About Cleveland versus Cincinnati, and about Timothy Hawkins needing a violin. If our budding romance—if one could call it that—was to succeed, we'd need to be open and honest with one another. Yet, what would motivate him to lie about such inconsequential things? It could be he was just forgetful or absent-minded. Weren't brilliant artists sometimes that way?

The telephone's shrill ring startled me. Moxie, dozing in a patch of sunlight, opened one eye in mild reproach.

"Mountain Melodies, Amanda Parrish speaking."

"Please hold." The operator paused, then said, "Go ahead."

"Amanda." Dieter's rich voice flowed through the receiver. "I trust I find you well?"

My heart did a little skip. "Yes, quite well, thank you."

"I am afraid I must beg your forgiveness." His accent caressed each word. "I had hoped to escort you to the concert this evening, but some of the young musicians require extra attention before the performance. You understand, of course? The pursuit of perfection demands sacrifices."

"Of course." I tried not to sound disappointed. "The concert must come first."

"Ah, but I was thinking..." A dramatic pause. "Perhaps afterward, we might celebrate? I know a charming spot by the lake where the moonlight dances on the water like silver notes in a nocturne."

I caught myself twirling the telephone cord around my finger like a schoolgirl. "That sounds lovely."

"Excellent!" His enthusiasm was infectious. "Then I shall count the minutes until I see your beautiful face in the audience. You will be there, yes? I am sorry you shall have to ride up in the camp wagon."

"I wouldn't miss it for the world." I was glad he couldn't see my flushed cheeks. "And you needn't worry about me. I'll ask James—Sheriff Holcomb—to give me a lift."

Was it my imagination, or did his tone cool slightly? "The good sheriff. How... convenient. Until tonight then, my dear Amanda."

"Until tonight."

After hanging up, I stood for a moment, savoring the lingering warmth of his voice. Moxie let out a disapproving meow.

"Oh, hush," I told him. "You just don't like competition for my affection."

As I returned to the ledger, I hummed a romantic waltz. The evening promised to be magical, even if it didn't start quite the way I'd hoped. And I'd have plenty of time to ask my questions... at the lake, under the moonlight.

Even so, a small internal voice nagged at me. *Be careful*, it whispered. *Things are not always as they seem.*

Chapter Nineteen

That evening, the grandfather clock in the hallway chimed seven times, its resonant tones echoing through the quiet house. I smoothed my dress for the umpteenth time, glancing out the window for any sign of the sheriff's automobile. He was running late. Maybe I should have taken the camp wagon, after all.

The anticipation of the concert at Camp Harmony tingled in my veins, mingled with a touch of anxiety for Molly, who had left earlier with that beautiful violin. After practicing with it all the previous evening, she decided she was comfortable enough to play it in the concert instead of the one borrowed from Rose. She'd worked very hard on her solo—that she didn't know I knew about—and I prayed it would go well for her.

To calm my nerves while waiting for James, I picked up the biography of Tchaikovsky that Dieter had lent me. I was only a few chapters in, but so far, the book had been a fascinating read, full of insights into the composer's life and work. I found a blank store receipt, now pressed into service as a bookmark, and picked up where I'd left off. Then something caught my eye when I turned the page. My breath hitched.

There, in the margin next to some fact about St. Petersburg, was a handwritten note. "Neva River," it said. "Rowboat. Lights from house."

It wasn't the content of the note that captured my attention. It was the handwriting. The elegant, precise script. The distinctive capital letters.

It was the same handwriting that was on the scrap of asylum stationery I'd found in the crate with Robert's violin.

To test this troubling theory, I yanked open the desk drawer, pulled out the note, and compared it to the writing in the margin of the book. No mistake. It was written by the same hand.

Had Dieter Volkov written the note from inside the Northern Illinois Asylum? But why would he have been—

My mind reeled as two random but distinct memories collided.

The first was the *Metronome* article about the young prodigy, Lucas Baker, who'd been institutionalized after attacking Imogene Lansdorf in an attempt to steal back the violin he still thought of as his. Where had he been incarcerated? The article didn't say. But since the crime had taken place in Chicago, the logical place for him to be sent would have been the Northern Illinois Asylum.

And the second memory was the photograph of Bobby and Luke taken at the World's Fair.

Could 'Luke' be Lucas Baker? and could 'Lucas Baker' be—

With trembling fingers, I reached back into the drawer and pulled out the old photograph. As I stared at the image of the two young men, a horrifying realization dawned on me.

The reason Lucas Baker had looked so familiar wasn't because of some vague resemblance to someone I'd known back in my student days. No, I knew exactly why he looked familiar.

Lucas Baker was a decades-younger version of Dieter Volkov.

How had I not seen this before?

But he told me he'd never been to Chicago. As if that minor detail mattered in the face of such enormous implications.

The room spun as the pieces fell into place. It wasn't Ernie or Camille Weiss who had been institutionalized at the asylum, nor even Robert—it was Dieter.

Or rather, Lucas Baker.

"Oh, my goodness." I gripped the edge of the desk for support. Dieter wasn't a Russian aristocrat at all. He was Lucas Baker, the child prodigy from Chicago. The prodigy who'd been institutionalized after attacking a woman.

The implications of this revelation crashed over me like a tidal wave. If Dieter was really Lucas Baker, then everything he'd told me about his past was a lie. Not just the fibs about never having seen Chicago, or about whether he called Cleveland or Cincinnati home. Of highest importance was the fact that, if he was the Lucas Baker from the article, then he was the one who had attacked Imogene Lansdorf all those years ago, trying to steal back his beloved violin.

A violin that was now in Molly's hands, on its way to Camp Harmony. And she had no idea. None.

My heart hammered in my chest. I had to warn her, to stop her from playing that violin in front of Dieter—in front of Lucas—until we got everything straightened out.

Just then, I heard the noisy *putt-putt* outside as James's Dodge pulled to the curb. I grabbed my purse. the note, and the photograph. I had to tell James everything on the way to the camp.

We must stop Dieter before he can harm Molly.

As I rushed out the door, I sent up a silent prayer for Molly's safety. The grand finale was about to become far more dramatic than anyone could have imagined.

Chapter Twenty

The Dodge rumbled up the winding mountain road, its headlights cutting through the gathering dusk. James clutched the wheel and stared straight ahead while I finished explaining my shocking discovery.

"So you're telling me that Dieter Volkov is actually Lucas Baker?" His voice strained with disbelief. "The same Lucas Baker who attacked Imogene Lansdorf over a violin back in 1893?"

I gripped the damning photograph in my trembling hands. "Yes, I think so. You'll see the resemblance, too. I'll show you the photo when we get there. If he's truly the 'Luke' in the photo, then we know he was present at the World's Fair, where Imogene Lansdorf performed. We found a souvenir program to her concert in one of Ernie's boxes. Remember? Molly and I made fun of her hat. Anyway, Lucas was desperate to get his violin back at any cost. And that violin is the very one Molly took for her performance tonight."

"But what about the Russian accent? 'Lucas Baker' doesn't sound very Russian to me."

"It's not. Molly tried to tell me the accent was phony. That everything about Dieter is phony. James, we have to hurry. She could be in danger!"

"But how did the violin end up with Molly? And is there any

connection between the violin and Ernie and Heidi?"

"I think I've pieced it together." My thoughts whirled in a crazy carousel. "Robert Weiss must have been Lucas's accomplice that night at the World's Fair. When Lucas got arrested after attacking Imogene Lansdorf, Robert escaped with the violin—which is a Strad, no less, according to the article in *Metronome*."

"What's a Strad?"

"A Stradivarius. A very, very valuable violin. Worth thousands, if not millions."

James released a low whistle. "But why didn't Robert just give the violin back to Lucas?"

"He couldn't," I explained. "Lucas was thrown in jail, then institutionalized in the asylum. That note we found with the violin—it must have been Lucas's instructions for Robert to keep it safe until he was released. Not that Robert could have sold it, anyway. Any dealer at the time would have recognized its value, heard of the theft, and realized it was stolen property."

"But the repairman you took it to didn't recognize its value," James reasoned. "And he was supposed to be an expert."

"No, it was in pretty sad shape. But Floyd did seem to indicate there was something special about the instrument. Something he wanted to check out with his colleague in Boston. I wish I'd pressed him to be more specific."

"Maybe he didn't want to get your hopes up, in case it was a forgery."

"Yes, that happens a lot in the violin market. There are hundreds of fake Strads floating around. Dealers need to be cautious."

"And you didn't suspect it when you saw it."

"Why, no. I mean, it seemed like a high-quality instrument, but there was no maker's mark or inscription on the inside. I just thought it was a lovely violin. Floyd's the expert. He would have known the telltale signs to look for, even without the label inside. But even he wasn't able to tell right away. Not without checking it further with his colleague."

James's jaw was set. "So when Robert died, the violin got shipped to Ernie with the rest of his belongings."

"Exactly," I continued. "But Ernie never went through those crates. They just sat in his shed for years. When Dieter—I mean, Lucas—came to town, he must have gone looking for it. He ransacked Ernie's house top to bottom, but must not have know about the shed. He either pushed Ernie down the stairs, or Ernie fell in the confusion." I paused. "I just thought of something else. The loud argument at Ernie's that Mildred Abernathy overheard—that could have been Lucas as well, insisting Ernie return the violin."

"Mildred said the man sounded 'tough.' She didn't mention a foreign accent."

"Don't you see? Dieter would have dropped the fake Russian accent whenever he was showing up as Lucas."

James uttered a mild expletive. "And Heidi?"

"When Lucas didn't find the violin at Ernie's he must have figured it went to Elite Repeat with the rest of Ernie's things. By then, I had already taken possession of it, but he didn't know that. Heidi must have surprised him during his search, and he..." I couldn't finish the sentence.

"He attacked her," James said. "And then scrawled that bigoted message on the wall to throw us off the scent."

"It was the perfect cover," I said bitterly. "No one would suspect him of such an anti-foreigner crime when he was posing as a foreigner himself. He took advantage of the vandalism wave. Maybe even vandalized the camp himself, to misdirect us."

We lapsed into a tense silence, the gravity of the situation weighing heavily upon us. The trees whipped by outside, their shadows dancing in the headlights.

"We'll get there in time, Amanda." James reached over to give my hand a reassuring squeeze. "We'll stop him."

I squeezed back, willing myself to believe him.

James gunned the engine as we raced up the mountain, but even at top speed, the Dodge could only go so fast on the rutted road. My mind raced faster than the automobile. I had to get to Molly before Lucas did something terrible.

We rounded the final bend and the lights of Camp Harmony came into view. Somewhere in that cheerful glow, Molly was preparing to play a priceless Stradivarius for a man willing to kill to possess it. Music drifted from the outdoor amphitheater—the concert had already started. James parked and we hurried toward the stage.

I grabbed his arm. "Wait. We need a plan. If we just rush in there, Lucas might panic and hurt someone."

James nodded. "What do you suggest?"

I thought quickly. "The stage has two wings. You take the left, I'll take the right. I know the program—Molly's solo is near the end of the first half. When she steps forward to play, that's when Lucas will recognize the violin. Who knows how he'll react? We need to be ready."

"What are you thinking?"

"I'm going to create a distraction. When I do, you grab Lucas."

"Amanda, that's too dangerous. Let me handle this."

"No time to argue." I spotted Clarence Butterworth in the wings, trumpet in hand. Perfect.

I hurried over to him. "Clarence, I need your help. When Molly starts her solo, Lucas—I mean, Maestro Volkov—might try to seize her violin. Can you help stop him?"

Clarence's eyes bugged out behind his glasses, but if he doubted my words, it didn't show. He squared his skinny shoulders. "Yes, ma'am. What should I do?"

I quickly outlined my plan. He nodded, face determined.

I took my position and waited through the seemingly interminable early part of the program until Molly stepped forward for her solo. The precious Stradivarius gleamed under the lights as she tucked it beneath her chin. My heart hammered.

The first pure, golden notes poured forth. Lucas stiffened at his podium, then slowly turned. I saw the exact moment he recognized his beloved violin. His face transformed from the cultured mask of Dieter into something wild and desperate.

Before he could move, I stepped out of the wings. "Is this what you're looking for, Lucas?" I called, holding up the photograph of him and Robert at the World's Fair.

He dropped the baton and froze. His fake accent slipped as he growled, "Where did you get that?"

The orchestra's playing faltered, as did Molly's. She stared at me as if I'd lost my marbles.

"From Robert's things. You remember Robert Weiss? Ernie's son, and your partner in crime?"

The audience and the orchestra members murmured in confusion. Lucas growled, "Give me that violin. It's mine!"

"No." I took another step toward him. "It belongs to Imogene Lansdorf's family. Just like it did when you attacked her in 1893."

With a primal roar, he lunged toward Molly. to her credit, my quick-thinking niece didn't hesitate. She tucked the Stradivarius under her arm like a football and took off, her long skirt hitched up to her knees. Lucas was right on her heels, his face contorted with manic desperation.

But Clarence was ready. As Lucas passed, Clarence stuck out his foot. The would-be violin thief went sprawling face-first into a tuba with a resonant "OOMPH!"

James was on him in a flash, snapping handcuffs around his wrists. "Lucas Baker, you're under arrest."

I ran to Molly, who was trembling but unharmed. "Oh, sweetheart." I pulled her close. "Are you all right?"

She nodded against my shoulder. "I'm fine. But I don't understand—what just happened?"

"A long story," I said. "one that started at the Chicago World's Fair and ended right here in Timber Coulee."

From his seat in the audience, Floyd Hendricks materialized, panting and disheveled. "Miss Parrish, I've been trying to reach you. My contact in Boston confirmed it—that violin is the Lansdorf Stradivarius!"

"We know," I said. "and now, thanks to Ernie's old photograph and some careful detective work, we've caught the man who's been hunting it all these years."

Floyd stretched out his hands. "Miss Mulroney," he murmured. "I hate to ask, but may I?" He gestured to the violin she still clutched to her chest.

With a questioning look at me, Molly handed over the Stradivarius. Floyd cradled it with reverence and awe, his eyes misty. "After all these years," he whispered. "The Lansdorf Stradivarius, safe at last."

As James led a ranting Lucas away, relief mixed with lingering adrenaline forced a laugh from my throat. "Well," I said, squeezing Molly's shoulders, "I'd say this little performance hit all the right notes—and then some!"

Molly groaned at my pun, but her eyes twinkled. "I can't believe

I've been playing a Stradivarius. No wonder it sounded so beautiful."

"Indeed." I looked over at Clarence, who was hovering nearby. "And speaking of beautiful things, I believe someone here deserves our thanks for his quick thinking."

Clarence blushed furiously as Molly turned to him with shining eyes. "My hero," she said, and the poor boy looked ready to faint from happiness.

I caught James's eye across the chaos. He winked, and a warmth that had nothing to do with the summer evening spread through my chest. Something told me that, while this particular mystery had been solved, a new movement in the symphony of my life was just beginning.

But first, we had some explaining to do to the good people of Timber Coulee. After all, one can't have a maestro arrested in the middle of the grand finale concert without owing folks a proper explanation.

Chapter Twenty-One

After an impromptu intermission to restore order and calm the audience, during which a hurried conference took place among the musicians on the stage, the grand finale concert resumed. The first-chair violinist took over at the podium as conductor. I suspected Molly might be too shaken up to play her solo, but as it turned out, I'd once again underestimated her. She rose to the occasion, tucked the renowned Stradivarius under her chin, and turned in a stellar performance before an awestruck crowd.

"What else could I do?" she asked me later. "I knew I'd never get another chance like this one during my lifetime." And all who were in attendance agreed that it was the most memorable concert in the history of Camp Harmony.

On Sunday afternoon, James stood in front of the Timber Coulee Town Hall, his uniform pressed for the occasion. Sunlight glinted off the star pinned to his chest. News had spread about the previous night's debacle, and a crowd had gathered, buzzing with excitement and relief.

Molly and I stood to one side, along with Floyd, the latter clutching the Stradivarius as if it might sprout wings and fly away.

James cleared his throat, silencing the crowd. "Ladies and gentlemen, I'm pleased to announce that the case of the Elite Repeat attack and the subsequent... er, attempted violin-napping... have been solved."

A smattering of applause broke out, quickly hushed by curious onlookers.

"The man known to us as Dieter Volkov is, in reality, Lucas Baker, a former child prodigy turned criminal." James paused to let the shocked murmuring die down. "It turns out our maestro was more interested in grand larceny than grand symphonies."

I leaned toward Molly. "You mistrusted him from the start," I whispered. "You and Moxie. Good instincts, both of you."

"Must run in the family," she whispered back.

I squeezed her hand. Under normal circumstances, I might have agreed. But blinded by Dieter's charming persona, I'd let my guard down. Never again.

James continued, "Baker and his accomplice stole the Stradivarius violin from the famous Imogene Lansdorf back in 1893." He turned to Floyd. "Mr. Hendricks, could you please tell us a little about the violin?"

Floyd stepped forward, cradling it in his arms. "For those who don't know, Antoni Stradivari made violins, and other stringed instruments, in the late seventeenth and early eighteenth centuries. His instruments are considered among the finest ever made. Approximately six hundred and fifty of his instruments survive in the world today, but countless fakes and counterfeits have flooded the market. We are pleased to say that this one is a confirmed original."

The crowd murmured in awe as Floyd stepped back and James resumed his account.

"Baker spent some twenty years in the state hospital at Elgin, Illinois. After managing to convince the doctors he was cured, he was released, changed his identity to that of Dieter Volkov, and started tracking down the violin. By that time, his accomplice, Robert Weiss, had died, but a recent article and photograph in *Metronome* magazine—widely read by musicians from coast to coast—led Lucas to seek out Robert's father, Ernie—may he rest in peace—here in Timber Coulee."

Gasps and mumbled remarks rippled through the crowd. I closed my eyes, my heart aching for Ernie. He never knew. All those years, and he never knew the treasure hidden in his own shed.

"But how did Lucas Baker come to be hired by the camp?" a man shouted. "Don't the Tates pay any attention to who they're hiring up there?"

Before James could respond, an urgent need to defend my friends propelled me forward.

"The Tates were caught in a bind when Stuart von Bauer canceled his participation at the last minute. Dieter—I mean, Lucas Baker stepped forward and seemed to have all the necessary qualifications to do the job, including great musical ability. Of course, they couldn't have possibly known he wasn't who he claimed to be."

"That's right, Amanda." James gave me a look that said *I've got it from here*. "On that aspect, we've been in touch with authorities in New York who've informed us that medical tests performed on Stuart von Bauer revealed traces of arsenic in his bloodstream. Mr. von Bauer was not merely ill. He was poisoned. In fact, he's lucky to be alive. His secretary told the police that, shortly before he became ill, a Russian violinist from out of town paid him a professional call and the two dined together. Detectives are now investigating the very real possibility that Baker might have poisoned the conductor, probably to incapacitate him and then offer himself for the position at Camp

Harmony, assuming the camp would be desperate for a replacement so close to opening for the season."

More gasps arose from the crowd. Molly looked at me and mouthed *Poisoned?* My stomach roiled as shock mixed with shame for being so blind to Dieter/Lucas's devious nature. I'd thought the faux maestro was brilliant, but not *that* brilliant. The great pains he'd taken to gain access first to Timber Coulee, then to Ernie, and finally to the violin defied belief. If only he could have used that razor-sharp mind of his to do something positive instead of leaving chaos and sorrow in his wake.

James was still speaking. "Yes, folks, our beloved handyman was unwittingly harboring a priceless instrument. But Ernie defended himself against Lucas, and ... well, Lucas couldn't risk being exposed. Whether Ernie fell down those stairs or was pushed ... Lucas is bound to illuminate us, sooner or later. As for Heidi Fischer, learning that Ernie's household belongings had gone to Elite Repeat, Lucas assumed his violin had been among them. When he burglarized her shop in search of it, she surprised him, and he attacked her."

"And thus his interest in *my* shop," I whispered to Molly. "All his questions for me about whether I stocked antique violins, and whether I had a spare violin lying around for Timothy, who didn't actually need one...Why, he must have pulled Timothy's name out of thin air." My voice faltered. *Lies. All lies.*

Mrs. Abernathy, her face red with indignation, piped up, "But what about all that German business? The writing on the wall?"

Agent Callaway stepped forward. "That's precisely what led us to the real criminals. I'm happy to say Oscar Barrington and Leon Danvers are locked up in the courthouse jail. Those two have been working as spies for the German government, using the planned hotel as a base to monitor railroad activity and intercept military communications. They've been working for a master operative called Simon, and we've been tracking their operation for months. Needless to say, the hotel will not be built, and the homeowners can rest easy that their properties remain secure."

Amid more appalled murmurs from the crowd, I raised my hand. "What about Oscar's boy, Rodney? And the other boys? Will they be tried for espionage, too?"

"No," the agent explained. "They are minors, and we have no reason to believe any of them had knowledge of the espionage activities. They are, however, being held responsible for the acts of vandalism."

"And Ernie?" Mrs. Wasserman asked.

"A hero," Callaway declared. "He was working with U.S. intelligence, hiding clues about their operation in his songbook." He looked at me with respect. "Those peculiar lyrics in his notebook weren't ravings, Miss Parrish. They were coded messages."

So I was right. I accepted the agent's unspoken apology with good grace. After all, who would have suspected sweet old Ernie of working for the government as a counter-spy? Certainly not I, had the lyrics in his notebook not seemed so odd. Which reminded me, I'd still need to come up with something for the Mountain Meadowlarks to sing. I wondered how "Signals in the Night" would strike them.

James's expression was grave. "Meanwhile, Baker used the current ... er, international tensions ... to misdirect our investigation and remove himself from suspicion. I'm afraid we all fell for it, hook, line, and sinker."

"Sheriff, if I may?" At James's nod, I stepped forward and addressed the crowd. "Neighbors, friends, this terrible affair has shown us the danger of letting fear and suspicion divide us. Heidi Fischer, Mrs. Wasserman, and everyone else are as much a part of Timber Coulee as any of us, regardless of their heritage. Let's honor Ernie's memory by coming together, not falling apart."

A murmur of agreement swept through the assembly.

James cleared his throat again. "Well said, Amanda. As sheriff of this county, I want to reassure all residents, wherever you might have come from, that acts of vandalism and personal harassment will not be tolerated. Let's all maintain a calm and considerate attitude toward one another without regard to nationality."

"What happens now?" someone asked.

"Lucas Baker is in custody and will likely be sent back to the asylum," James said. "Now, as for the Stradivarius, it will be returned to Imogene Lansdorf's heirs, as she passed away some years ago, never knowing what happened to her precious violin. And Camp Harmony will carry on as usual next year, its twenty-sixth season. With a change in musical direction, of course."

Molly raised her hand. "Do you think Mrs. Lansdorf's family might be willing to sell the violin?"

"They might. Does anyone here have a spare million dollars lying around?"

"Rats." Molly gave a theatrical sigh. "I knew I shouldn't have spent my last million on Mrs. Wasserman's almond crescents."

Laughter rippled through the crowd, the tension of the past days breaking at last.

As the townspeople began to disperse, James's eyes met mine. A flutter arose in my chest that had nothing to do with the case we'd just solved.

He turned to talk to a reporter, and I linked arms with my niece. "Well, Molly-girl, I'd say this has been quite the eventful summer vacation. Perhaps next year we'll stick to something less exciting. How does a nice, quiet knitting circle sound?"

Molly snorted. "Only if we're knitting bulletproof waistcoats. I have a feeling trouble has a way of finding us."

I tugged her sleeve, steering us toward home. "Come on. I think we've earned ourselves a large slice of pie and an even larger pot of tea."

Walking home, talking about the events of the past few days, I found myself wondering what Dieter would think of it all. But Dieter didn't exist. He was a phantom, a falsehood, no more substantial than mist.

Molly's wistful voice broke into my thoughts. "I'm sorry the camp season is over, in spite of everything. I had fun."

"Me too."

"Who do you think will be next year's conductor?"

"The board will have to discuss it, but I'm going to suggest we extend another invitation to Stuart von Bauer. If we can convince him to come, then maybe I'll be able to unload those records, after all."

The inescapable fact that her summer break would soon be ending cast a shadow over my mood. I unlocked the front door, and we flung off our hats and collapsed onto the sofa. "Molly, I've been thinking. There's no sense in your returning to the conservatory with that broken violin, and we need to give the borrowed one back to Rose. Why don't you let me send you a brand-new instrument when the shipment comes in? Unless it arrives before you leave, in which case, you can have your pick. It would be my way of saying thank-you for all your hard work in the shop."

"That's very kind of you, Aunt Amanda, but I've been thinking, too ..."

Her expression was serious, as was her voice. "What is it, sweetie?"

She took a deep breath. "I ... I don't want to go back to Chicago."

"You don't?" I shifted on the sofa to see her face, but couldn't read her expression.

Her lips curved into a gentle arc. "No. I'd like to stay here in Timber

Coulee, if that's all right with you. I want to keep working at Mountain Melodies and ... well, keep living with you and Moxie."

My heart swelled with joy, but I sought to keep my voice steady. "What about the conservatory? Your musical career?"

"To be honest, I never really wanted to be a professional musician. I love music, but the conservatory was just ... something to do, so I wouldn't have to live on the farm forever. But here, in Timber Coulee, I feel like I've found a real home."

My mind whirled. "Of course, I'm flattered. But—"

"But what?"

"Have you considered what your parents will say? They might object to your not returning home. Your mother, especially." My sister Kathleen had always thought I was too independent for my own good. I didn't need her accusing me of having a negative influence on her impressionable daughter.

"I wouldn't worry about them. They both know I'm not cut out for farm life. Papa's mostly concerned that I find some secure way to earn a living. And Mother—well, she'd prefer I follow a more traditional path and land myself a husband."

"As any mother would." Including my own, who'd waited—not always patiently—for me to "come to my senses" and settle down.

"I'd like that, too," Molly said. "But I haven't met any suitable candidates up to this point, and I'm not the kind of girl to just sit around, waiting. So I thought..." Her sidelong glance at me carried a glint of uncertainty. "Well, it was just an idea..."

Unable to contain my excitement any longer, I pulled her into a fierce hug. "Oh, my dear girl! Nothing would make me happier than to have you stay."

Joy blossomed across her face. "Really?" She returned my hug. "You're sure I won't be in the way?"

I pulled back, keeping my hands on her shoulders. "In the way? Nonsense. I've loved having you here. And Moxie has too, haven't you, you old softie?"

Moxie meowed in what I chose to interpret as agreement.

"But you're going to have to write to your parents and get their permission to leave the conservatory."

"I will. I'm sure they'll be ecstatic, as long as I'm under your wing."

Ecstatic might not have been the word I'd chosen, but no matter. If my sister turned out to be less than pleased about the arrangement, she'd let me know in short order. In the meantime, my wing looked forward to sheltering a chick.

A mischievous thought occurred to me. "You know, Molly." I tried to keep my tone casual. "I can't help but wonder if your decision might have something to do with a certain young man who plays the trumpet?"

Molly's cheeks flushed a delightful shade of pink. "Aunt Amanda! I... well... maybe Clarence might have factored into my decision. A little."

I gave her a knowing wink. "Just a little, hmm?"

"Oh, stop it." Molly gave my arm a playful swat. "Clarence is sweet, and talented, and ... well, we'll see what happens."

My heart filled to bursting with happiness and hope for Molly's future. "Indeed we will. Now, come on. This calls for a celebration. Let's keep the shop closed this afternoon and go get some of Mrs. Wasserman's almond crescents."

"You'll get no argument from me." She linked her arm through mine.

As we put on our hats, Moxie wound himself around our ankles, meowing plaintively.

"Oh, don't worry, your majesty," I laughed, scratching behind his ears. "I'm sure Mrs. Wasserman will have a bit of cream for her favorite customer. She always does."

Moxie's purr rumbled like distant thunder as he padded ahead of us to the door, tail held high like a flagpole. He'd appointed himself our escort ever since the incident with Lucas, as if determined not to let us out of his sight again. Perhaps he'd known all along—cats do have a way of sensing these things.

We stepped out into the warm evening air, Moxie trotting between us with regal dignity. A profound sense of contentment settled over me. My little family—Molly, Moxie, and me—was complete. For now. And who knew? Perhaps someday soon we might be adding a certain trumpeter—or a certain sheriff—to our merry band.

Timber Coulee had weathered its share of storms this summer, but as we strolled down the street, the setting sun painting the sky in vibrant hues of pink and gold, I knew that brighter days were ahead.

Whatever the future might bring, we'd face it together, one measure at a time.

And Moxie, with his approving purr, seemed to agree.

The End

Author's Note

While *Murder on a High Note* is a work of fiction, a couple of real-life historical situations provided inspiration for this story.

"Violin-napping" is a real thing. Stradivarius violins in particular seem to present a near-irresistible challenge to thieves, even though they are practically impossible to resell, because anyone knowledgeable of the value of such an instrument would also likely know it was stolen property. Many cases remain unsolved, though one recent, encouraging example is the theft and eventual return (after thirty-five years) of the Ames-Totenberg Stradivarius.

During World War I, German Americans faced widespread persecution. In my Midwestern hometown, a German-owned bakery was vandalized, like Mrs. Wasserman's. Communities banned German language classes and church services. Sauerkraut became "liberty cabbage" and hamburgers became "liberty sandwiches." In some cases, German Americans were subjected to surveillance, mob violence, and even internment. Across history, fear has led people to turn against their innocent neighbors, yet the gospel of Jesus Christ gives us hope that we can learn to respond with greater wisdom and compassion.

In Gratitude

To God be the glory.

I offer my deepest thanks to:

Pegg Thomas, patient editor and storyteller *par excellence*;

Anita Aurit, Terese Luikens, and Grace Robinson, cherished writer friends and all-around smart cookies;

Linda Nelson, first reader *extraordinaire*;

The women of the Thursday night Bible study at Kootenai Church;

And especially my husband, Thomas Leo, for his steadfast love and encouragement.

And thanks to you, dear reader, for taking a chance on my book. Please visit my website at JenniferLamontLeo.com to sign up for my Reader Community or drop me a line. I'd love to hear from you!

Also by Jennifer Lamont Leo

The Corrigan Sisters Series

You're the Cream in My Coffee

Ain't Misbehavin'

Wrap Your Troubles in Dreams

The Windy City Hearts Series

Moondrop Miracle

The Rose Keeper

Love's Grand Sweet Song

The Music Shop Mysteries Series

Murder on a High Note

Something Wicked This Way Hums

Snake in the Brass (*coming 2025*)

Novellas

"Undercover Logger" in *Lumberjacks and Ladies* (Barbour Publishing)

"The Violinist" in *The Highlanders* (Iron Stream Media)

Sneak Peek

Book Two in the Music Shop Mysteries series

Coming up next in the Music Shop Mysteries series . . .
SOMETHING WICKED THIS WAY HUMS

As the Great War rages overseas, the Rocky Mountain Meadowlarks Ladies' Choral and Knitting Society is rehearsing for their Liberty Bond concert. But when a longtime choir member is found murdered, amateur sleuth Amanda Parrish must determine whether the discord stems from a heated rivalry between two sopranos or something far more sinister. Can she and Molly race to uncover the truth before another voice is silenced forever?

What's the Buzz?

Reviews are pure gold to an author! If you enjoyed this book and want to help spread the word, post reviews on book-oriented websites like Amazon, Goodreads, and BookBub. Reviews can be short or as long as you like. And please talk about the book, in person and on social media. Word-of-mouth is still the best way to promote just about anything!

Let's stay in touch. Please stop by and say hello.

JenniferLamontLeo.com (Join my Reader Community for book news, exclusive content, and more)

Facebook

Goodreads

Amazon

A Sparkling Vintage Life (My podcast! Listen online at sparklingvintagelife.com or subscribe in your favorite podcast app)